WHAT PEOPLE ARE S

GAG

Gag is the most unsettling and unexpected of Parisian love stories. It examines two characters whose secrets bind them together rather then keep them apart. I was unable to put *Gag* down with its Martin Amis like acerbic wit and constantly surprising turn of events. It's a sour little morsel, but one you can't help but devour.
Christina Wayne, CEO Assembly Entertainment, television producer and executive: Mad Men, Breaking Bad, Copper and Broken Trail

Gag is a delectably twisted version of the American-in-Paris story; a tale of hurt, loss, redemption and love, where damaged people collide... The plot careens from one surprising turn to another, keeping the reader enthralled until the last, crazy, heart-breaking page.
Mira Kamdar, author of the award-winning memoir *Motiba's Tattoos* and the critically acclaimed *Planet India*

Melissa Unger is an important new voice in modern fiction... She picks up where Camus left off ... her work is astonishing both in its nod to the history of literature and in its incredible originality. Read this and be amazed.
Stacy London, author of the *New York Times* bestselling book, *The Truth About Style*. Co-host of the popular television show What Not to Wear

Unger's Kafka-esque tale sweeps from Brooklyn to Paris to points Beyond, into a strange new world which grows stranger by the page.

Charles Graeber, award-winning journalist and *New York Times* bestselling author of *The Good Nurse: A True Story of Medicine, Madness, and Murder*

Gag

Gag

Melissa Unger

Winchester, UK
Washington, USA

First published by Roundfire Books, 2014
Roundfire Books is an imprint of John Hunt Publishing Ltd., Laurel House, Station Approach,
Alresford, Hants, SO24 9JH, UK
office1@jhpbooks.net
www.johnhuntpublishing.com
www.roundfire-books.com

For distributor details and how to order please visit the 'Ordering' section on our website.

ISBN: 978 1 78279 564 3

A CIP catalogue record for this book is available from the British Library.

Design: Stuart Davies
www.stuartdaviesart.com

Cover image: Emma Strangwayes-Booth

Printed and bound by CPI Group (UK) Ltd, Croydon, CR0 4YY

Gag is dedicated to those among you who have a way of seeing and being in the world that no one else understands.

Do not kneel to the norm, do not swallow your words and do not give up your vision. Follow your own path unhindered by what others think or say.

Blessed are the cracked, for they shall let in the light.
-Groucho Marx

-1

Peter Howland never ate. It was a secret he guarded with great care and agility. A writer, he was able to bend the reality of his work hours to accommodate his condition. His friends never suspected anything out of the ordinary. Arriving always after dinner, meeting only for drinks or coffee. Most assumed he had just eaten with someone else, others simply thought he was broke and understandably too proud to accept their repeated offers to foot his bill. In truth, Peter had given up food completely about fifteen years ago at the age of twenty-two. Finally freed from the constraints of parental supervision and the structured mealtimes of school and college, Peter happily left behind an action he had never enjoyed. The repulsive smells and textures, the ceaseless, monotonous chewing, the troublesome after effects of indigestion and gas, were all stopped for good, one rainy afternoon in a Brooklyn diner when Peter punctured a poached egg with his fork. Undercooked, the egg oozed a thick, snot-like goo, he felt a gag reflex in the back of his throat, and pushed his plate away. He never ate again.

Peter's second and undoubtedly more astonishing secret was that although he had not ingested a morsel of food in over a decade, he had remarkably suffered no visible ill effects. He was fairly fit in a 'writing all day in a poorly lit room' kind of way, and weighed about average for a man of his height. He hadn't been sick since college, where he had gotten Mono from a girl who turned out to be the campus slut. He had never suffered from hunger pangs, not even at the start. Over time, he realized that he had never really felt hunger in his life; he simply ate reflexively, because he was told to.

Growing up as an only child in an upper-middle-class New York home, food had always been prepared for him. He had rolled out of bed to a breakfast of pancakes before heading off to school, where at lunchtime he dutifully joined his classmates in consuming the treats contained in the oversized chrome lunchbox his mother had brought back from a shopping trip to Milan. For dinner, he either ate with his parents or in front of the TV; either way, food was automatically put in front of him at a set time. In high school and college, as is American tradition, meals were also provided in the same regimented manner, so it wasn't until about a week after he had given up food completely, and he began to ponder how it could possibly be that he wasn't hungry, that he realized that he had in actuality, never been.

For the first few days after the egg incident, he was simply nauseated at the thought of food. *This is great,* he reasoned, pleased at the idea of losing some of the weight he had gained from all the pot he had smoked in college.

By day four, he thought to himself: *Well, I suppose I'd better eat something.*

He grabbed a piece of sliced bread, toasted it, dabbed on some grape jelly. He looked at it. It seemed innocuous enough; he lifted it to his lips. No go. He put it back on the plate, smelled it and tried again. No.

He went about his business for the rest of the day, which at that time consisted largely of browsing in record stores and masturbating. During the short breaks he took from both, he forced himself to think about food. There were a huge variety of victuals readily available in his neighborhood; as he passed the beckoning signs, he contemplated each one: *Pizza…no. Pad Thai…no. Sushi…no.* Nothing got his gastric juices flowing. Nothing.

About a week into it, he started to get nervous. Not hungry and not eating at all, he still felt totally fine. What the hell was happening? Much as he hated to, he thought he'd better see a doctor. He called his mother.

"Hi, Mom."

"What's wrong?"

"Nothing's wrong, Mom, can't I just call to say hi?"

"Oh, please."

"Don't start, Mom." He paused to light a cigarette. "Can I just have Dr. Gordon's number? I want him to have a look at me."

"Oh my God, Peter, not again! Does it burn when you pee?"

"Jesus Christ, Mom! Just give me the goddamn number!"

The next afternoon, he found himself sitting on Dr. Gordon's examining table. In her haste to clean up after the previous patient, the nurse had forgotten to pull down a fresh sheet of protective paper, and now his bare ass was sticking to the vinyl. He was sitting with his hands tucked under is butt cheeks when Dr. Gordon barged in without knocking.

"Hello, Peter," he said coldly. "I hear from your dad that you broke his boss's daughter's heart." He pulled on a latex glove with an exaggerated snap "…and her hymen too for that matter." He shook his head and took a deep breath. "None of my business I suppose... What can I do for you?"

Fuck you, old man, Peter thought to himself, but instead replied, "Haven't had a check-up in a while and I thought it might be a good idea to make sure that I was, you know...healthy."

"Are you using condoms?"

"Dr. Gordon," he said curtly. "It's nothing like that. I just want a full check-up. Okay?"

"Fine. I just assumed…well let's see, when was the last time we saw you?" he said, shuffling some paperwork with his ungloved left hand. "Hmm, about four years ago, the physical right before you went off to college I reckon."

"Yes, sir," Peter replied with exaggerated obsequiousness.

"Well, okay then, let's get started."

A half hour later, after being poked and prodded in every orifice, Dr. Gordon sent him on his way. He was completely healthy in every capacity – the doctor's one recommendation? Go easy on the food a little, lose a few pounds. Ha.

He went straight to the store and bought a scale. He hid it in his closet; he did not want his friends to think he was vain. He weighed himself – 170 lbs. He let four more days go by before weighing himself again, the scale's red needle stayed fixed firmly in place, taunting him like a raised middle finger. He looked in the mirror; he didn't even look tired.

He did a slow lap around the apartment, did a few push-ups and sat on the couch. Suddenly the enormity of it all overwhelmed him. He felt a surge of panic.

"I am alive and healthy and yet I do not ingest any foooooood!" he said out loud, stretching the o's dramatically.

"I enjoy beverages of all kinds; coffee, alcohol, soda," he continued in an overly mechanical voice. "I even indulge in cigarette smoking and drug taking. I ejaculate hardily.

"But..." he did a drum roll on the coffee table with his hands and shouted, "I do not eat...ANYTHING...AT ALL!!!!!!" And then as if to convince even himself, he added, pointedly, "Ever.

"Am I a freak? Am I an alien? Am I dead? Am I nuts?" he asked his lamp, provocatively. The lamp did not respond; he took it to be a good sign.

He cut his toenails. That usually relaxed him. It did not. He smoked some pot and drank a whiskey, actually: three. Didn't work either. He paced around the apartment again, then sat at his computer and typed: *How long can a human being survive without food?* Accounts and opinions seemed to vary. He read about the Donner Party, about the soccer team that crashed in the Andes, about miners trapped in caves, about Jesus.

Peter looked at himself in the mirror again, searching for something in his reflection that would clarify his condition.

He opened his mouth and wiggled his tongue. He swallowed theatrically. Chewed air. Conjured the tastes of his once favorite foods. No hunger.

He dropped to the ground and did another round of push-ups. He felt great.

"What the fuck?" he said simply.

He sat on the couch and reached for his lighter and held the flame against the palm of his left hand.

"Ouch."

Not dead.

"I can't tell anyone about this, can I?" he reasoned out loud. "They'll lock me up, cut me open," he added, dramatically.

He pictured himself touring the country like a freak in a cage, people throwing various foods at him, yelling *"Eat! Eat! EAT!"*

"This shit is simply not fucking possible! What the FUCK is going on?!" he yelled at the cactus in the corner of the room; its thick, green arms seemingly raised in a "search me, I dunno" gesture.

"Fuck you," he said to it, circling menacingly, spoiling for a fight.

Over the next few months, still without a morsel of food ever passing his lips, he studied, pondered, searched, for some sort of explanation. But none was forthcoming. On a number of occasions he considered discussing it with various friends. Once he nearly told his father, but did not. Walking down the street one afternoon, fear gripped him so forcefully that he vomited a small amount of thin, clear bile into the gutter.

With a determination he showed in no other areas of his life, he somehow managed to push the reality of his predicament out of his mind. One morning, weeks later still, leaning forward to look into the refrigerator, he allowed himself one final, faint hope that something would appeal to him. But realizing that he had passed the point of no return, he shut the heavy door definitively.

"Whatever," he simply said.

Eventually, his bowel movements ceased; and as he did not miss them, he simply adjusted, rather as he would have to a new haircut or a new city or a new job; gradually forgetting, over time, how life had been before that final egg.

In the fifteen years since, Peter had led a fairly mundane life; the years had slipped by quickly. Buoyed by the perfect combination of his parents' money and their disinterest, he had been free to live a very comfortable existence. Though still living in his first, post-collegiate apartment, the seedy Brooklyn neighborhood had developed around him into a gentrified haven of artists and hipsters, who had quickly become his friends. It was a perfect match, their lax, bohemian attitudes allowed him room to maneuver and easily miss meals, even canceling at the last minute. Without angering them he was able to retain a number of casual friendships. He wrote mediocre prose for a number of local literary magazines and had become a bit a cult figure for his combination of good looks, evasiveness and apparent disinterest in maintaining a love relationship with anyone of either sex. Now pushing forty, he was entering that danger zone where possibility gives way to improbability.

His slate blue eyes had started to have trouble focusing on the morning newspaper and his wavy, dark brown hair had recently gone to salt and pepper. He kept it a little long, thinking it made him look younger, in actuality, coupled with his delicate, even features, it made him look almost girlish. Many of the women he bedded hated waking up next to him – he always looked prettier than they did in the morning. Yet Peter had charmed a harem's worth of them into bed. He had become the king of late-night dating. Turning up at midnight with champagne and flowers, he drew bubble baths, read poetry…but inevitably, about a month in, the women always wanted more, the nocturnal romps had started to feel shallow and cheap. He'd buzz their buzzers hopefully, but they would all eventually refuse to let him in: "Take me out to a nice dinner, and then we'll see," they'd always say. Peter, without responding, would simply slink off into the night, never to be heard from again; easily camouflaging himself in the army of assholes they had dated in their lives.

He sometimes wondered how much the not eating had shaped

his life. It certainly had made him feel *special.* He'd wandered the Brooklyn streets feeling significantly superior. The only glitch was that he hadn't told anyone. If pressed as to why, he would likely have said something glib, like, "Hey baby, I may be a Zombie, my place or yours?" *That isn't much of an icebreaker, now is it? ... Best to keep secrets secret.*

But in truth, he was afraid. Afraid that if he spoke his secret aloud, that all the foodless years would catch up with him somehow, horror movie-style and collapse him into a pile of dust. To cope, he had spent the last fifteen years in a kind of sophomoric daze, often just forgetting how weird it all was. In essence, he had spent a large portion of his life vacillating between sheer panic and total denial. Haven't we all?

Until one morning, he woke abruptly. He was drenched in sweat. He sat up in bed and felt the back of his neck; his pillow had a circular ring of wet on it where his head had been. He looked around to get his bearings. His gaze was drawn to the food artfully placed around the apartment like props on a movie set. He was gripped by an intense and ineffable feeling. It was as if a curtain had been lifted to let the light in and reveal the veiled corners at the furthest reaches of his consciousness. His mind wandered back to the initial egg incident (OVO, as he secretly called it).

Wow, he thought, *fifteen fucking years, bet that beats all the records.*

He got out of bed and lit a cigarette.

"What the fuck am I going to do?" he said looking down into the glowing ember. He considered trying the old burn test again; instead, he called his mother.

"Hi, Mom".

"Our lawyer is on vacation in St. Barth's."

"What?"

"He's out of town. You're on your own."

"What the hell are you talking about?"

"Well, I assume you're in trouble."

"Christ, Mom. No," he answered angrily, and then softened his voice. "Well, not exactly. I just need to borrow a little extra money, a couple of *thou* over the usual monthly thing."

"Is she pregnant?"

"Oh for fuck's sake, Mom, no! I was just thinking I should take a little trip."

"I'll send the driver"

"No, Mom, further than that. I was thinking I would go to Paris for a few months."

"Paris?! You haven't set foot outside the five boroughs in fifteen years and now you want to go to Paris?! Are you nuts?"

"Possibly."

She sighed and continued. "I'm certain it's so profoundly uninteresting that I am I going to regret asking, but, Peter – what's going on?"

"I don't know, Mom, I… I just think it's time for me to get out of town."

"She's pregnant with twins!" she shouted, feigning delight.

"Mom!"

"Okay, fine, but why Paris?"

Peter took a breath to answer and then stopped. He actually had no real idea why. It was just a feeling…in his gut.

Irritated at having to justify himself, he mumbled, "It's far away, I need a big change and my French is decent from being raised by Mathilde..." He often used Mathilde, his parents' French housekeeper, as a weapon when he felt like hurting his mother.

"Mathilde didn't raise you," she interrupted.

He ignored her. "…Beyond that, I was thinking I could finally try to write something worthwhile."

"Well, you may not be nuts, but you certainly are very cliché."

"Thanks a lot, Mom. Aces," he said sarcastically.

"Peter, look, I've gotta go, I've a manicure in five minutes. Do whatever you want, I'll wire some money to your account."

He booked a ticket for the very next week. In his Brooklyn apartment, he simply threw out all of the things that might rot during his absence and left the rest as it was. While rifling through his drawers to pack a small bag for the trip, he felt a twinge of some unrecognizable emotion. The bras, sweaters, panties all left behind by different women, were jumbled in with his own clothes, suggesting a degree of communion that he had in actuality never experienced. That was certainly something the not eating had stolen from him: intimacy. But never having experienced it, he wasn't able to properly identify the numb, longing pinch he felt in his heart.

He did not tell his friends or acolytes about his impending departure, he secretly enjoyed propagating his enigmatic reputation. On his door, to dispel potential rumors of his death, he tacked a note that simply said: *Back in five.* Five minutes, months or years, he did not specify.

He went to say goodbye to his parents, not out of affection, but out of guilt for the money they were lending him. On his way to the airport, he looked out their limousine's window at the squat, ugly modern buildings and banality of Queens. He felt a surge of excitement; he held his brand new passport up to his lips. "Paris," he whispered to it.

He had been to Paris once before, during high school. He particularly remembered the Parisian pastry shops, how they seemed to be literally on every corner, how beautiful the windows were, how the desserts, tiny individual masterpieces, were lined up in rows like pretty little dolls waiting to be played with.

His gaze shifted to his own reflection in the tinted glass partition between him and the driver. "This is it, buddy," he said to himself, "you are heading into the belly of the beast, the gastronomic center of the universe." He felt like a superhero in disguise. The writing was to be a front; Peter was going to Paris to have another go at food.

1

Peter shuffled along obediently with his fellow passengers. Distracted, he bumped into the woman in front of him who shot him an annoyed glance over her shoulder and muttered something nasty under her breath in French. He smiled at her in exaggerated, ironic apology. He remembered that about Paris too: Assholes, everywhere.

"At least I'll fit right in," he laughed to himself.

He looked down at his boarding pass. *Seat 29 B (*despite his parents' generous offer, he had insisted on flying coach, it was his way of being subversive.) He hadn't flown since his teens. He felt something stir in the pit of his stomach. At first he thought it might be hunger, but then recognized it as fear.

Once on the plane, he settled into the bulkhead aisle seat his mother had told him to request.

"It is the only civilized way to endure coach," she had declared categorically.

The plane doors were about to close but the seat next to him was still empty. He wavered between wanting it to stay vacant so he could spread out, and wishing that a lovely available young woman might fill it. Even the most levelheaded of unattached travelers succumbs to this momentary hope. The potential excitement of romancing a stranger, the fate and serendipity of it all is just too alluring to resist. Instead, the inevitable happened: loud, fat, male and smelling slightly of refried beans.

"Hiya! Mind if I squeeze in there, buddy?"

Well of course I do, you bovine monster, Peter thought to himself, averting his gaze, repulsed; but he got up silently and let the man through.

Pretending to read, Peter stole glances at his burden out of the corner of his eye. The man was actually younger than he had first thought, maybe early thirties, very fat, but not obese; just sort of stretching the limits of fit's patience. He had reddish hair, accompanied by the expected ruddy complexion. Peter had been able to view the beast in his entirety when he had been asked to rise to help dispatch the man's obscenely heavy bag to the overhead bin. He was dressed all in black and had a distinct un-ironic, Johnny Cash-ness about him that made him look rather cool. Despite the beany odor, which was now growing more distinct, Peter relaxed a little.

After much shuffling, shifting and seatbelt adjusting, the man finally settled in, turned to Peter and bellowed.

"Dallas Foster," he said loudly, with a drawl. "The name's Dallas, I'm from Memphis, but my mom got knocked up in Dallas, so I'm stuck with it."

Peter noticed that despite his seeming lack of hygiene, that Dallas' teeth were exceptionally white. "Peter Howland, Brooklyn, New York".

Before more could be said, the captain announced the plane's impending departure and they began speeding down the jet way, as the wheels left the ground Peter involuntarily gripped his armrests.

"Nervous flyer?" Dallas inquired. "We'll get a drink in ya soon enough and you'll forget that we're airborne on a hunk of tin!"

Peter managed a condescending smile.

When the stewardess came by, Dallas ordered two beers for himself and Peter asked for a glass of red wine.

"Wine, huh? No siree, I'm a beer man myself. Where I come from wine comes in a box and it ain't too tasty."

He can't be for real, Peter thought to himself.

In the awkward silence, Dallas started eyeing Peter's unopened bag of peanuts.

"Would you like these?" Peter offered more in an effort to get him to look away than out of generosity.

"Yes, I would thank you. You not hungry?"

"I don't eat on planes, not my kind of food really, plus I read somewhere that it exacerbates jet lag." Peter was a pro at dodging such questions.

"Well it's lottery day for me then!! You just take that dinner when it comes, my friend, and I'll take it off your hands soon as the little sky waitress passes by. I'm starving!"

Peter cracked up. Guffawed actually. It surprised him. He didn't laugh spontaneously very much; a broody disposition went better with the persona he had cultivated for himself.

"I'm sorry, Dallas, I didn't mean to laugh, your....um...enthusiasm surprised me."

"Hey, buddy, that's okay, laughter is good for the soul."

"Yes it is, Dallas, yes it is," Peter said, actually meaning it, but was quickly embarrassed by the cheesiness of the moment and pretended to read.

When the dinners came, Dallas, true to his word, did indeed eat both, but much to Peter's surprise, he did not instigate conversation. Peter had thought for sure that mealtime would provide a convenient opening for Dallas to unfurl his whole life's story in excruciating yet colorful detail. Instead, Dallas put on his headphones and methodically worked his way through both trays (appetizer, appetizer, main course, main course, dessert, dessert) while staring vaguely ahead. Peter was disappointed. It was as if the promised entertainment had reneged on the gig. So while Dallas ate, he pointedly did the *New York Times* crossword puzzle, in ink. It was Friday and he completed the entire thing in the time it took Dallas to eat the two meals. Peter may have been a stoner in college, but he had had a lot of time to kill in coffee shops in the years since. He placed his finished masterpiece triumphantly on his tray table, angled subtly in Dallas' direction. After a few minutes, Dallas did indeed glance over, Peter readied himself to gloat about his intellectual prowess, Dallas' eyes lit up, he looked up at Peter, he pulled an ear clear of his headphones and asked sheepishly, "You gonna eat that?" pointing to the after-dinner chocolate the stewardess had placed by the newspaper on Peter's tray table.

Eventually, the cabin lights dimmed. Peter reached up,

squinting at its brightness and turned off the reading light above his head. He turned his upper torso away from Dallas, pulled the cheap synthetic blanket up to his chin and closed his eyes; projected onto the blackness behind each lid was the outline of an egg.

Soon the stewardess reached over both their bodies, to raise the blinds and the French sun came brightly pouring into the cabin. Wordlessly, because there was already an unspoken understanding between them, Dallas ate his way through both breakfasts (yogurt, yogurt, croissant, croissant, banana, banana).

Because he was taller, as they were getting ready to deplane, Peter helped Dallas bring his bag down from the bin above.

"Wow, this thing weighs a ton! What do you have in here?" said Peter picturing a severed head or some such backwoods horror.

"Tricks of the trade, my friend, tricks of the trade," Dallas replied, smiling enigmatically.

Since Peter had not been privy to anything about Dallas, other than the unfortunate origin of his name, he had no hint as to what that might be.

They deplaned single file, Peter behind Dallas, and remained in this loose formation until they reached the baggage claim, at which point Dallas veered off and headed toward the exit, a few steps later he seemed to remember something. He turned and walked straight toward Peter.

"Where are my manners? Thanks for dinner, buddy, and breakfast. Feels like I should put out or something." He laughed loudly. "Seeing you bought me dinner and all!" He shook his head to show he was only kidding and slapped Peter hard on the back. "Have a 'bonne' time in Paree, my friend."

Peter reached for his hand to shake it. Dallas seemed struck by the formality of the gesture and held Peter's gaze rather intently. For a second, Peter thought he saw a layer of something else in Dallas' eyes. Intelligence maybe. Then it was gone.

"Hope you manage to get yourself a little something sweet to eat while you're here!" Dallas yelled over his shoulder as he walked away grinning lasciviously. "If ya know what I mean. The sweet bit of stuff tastes better here than anywhere else in the world!" he drooled.

What a gross thing to yell at a stranger in an airport, Peter thought. *Vile.* Vile indeed; yet also unintentionally apt.

The apartment his parents had arranged for him, a *pied-a-terre* belonging to a business acquaintance of his father's, was located near the banks of the Seine in the Latin Quarter. Two keys had been left with the *gardienne*. A matched set. Paris *pied-a-terres* are often hideaways for lovers; this one clearly, was no exception. It was in a small, ancient, but lovely building and as he walked up the narrow, carpeted staircase towards the flat, he imagined the cozy, vintage gem that awaited him. A glorious, Technicolor slideshow of all the French women he would bed there flickered through his mind.

He turned the key in the door and pushed it open to instant disappointment. The place looked like a banal hotel suite at a Hilton in Denver. He had expected gently worn antiques, a four-poster bed perhaps, a quaint, Provence-inspired kitchen. Instead, he found furniture so ugly that he actually closed his eyes involuntarily for a second.

The couch, a monstrous, modern, ultra-suede eyesore was additionally insulting because it was teal. Peter hated teal, passionately, aggressively. He had once drunkenly orated for hours about this aversion to a group of friends, ending his tirade with, "Teal represents dishonesty and stupidity. It's a false color that doesn't exist in nature, its hypocritical, pledging allegiance to both green and blue, it's the worst humanity has to offer, that horrible combination of ignorance and aggressiveness, every time I see teal, I want to slap it." They had all laughed.

"Teal? Really? Teal?!" Peter said accusingly to the couch.

Two, brown *pleather* club chairs were plopped in front of it. Their cheap foam stuffing having taken on the shape of their sitters' asses and arms, they appeared almost amorphous, their plastic-y skin shimmered faintly in places and to Peter, they looked like freshly shat turds.

He tossed his bag onto the large, low, rectangular coffee table. It skidded across the hideous white and grey speckled Formica surface; he watched it slow to a halt on its far edge and then he guardedly proceeded into the bedroom.

"Good God," he gasped.

It was a small room and the bed took up most of it. The curtains and bedspread were mustard colored. He leaned down to touch the spread.

"What the hell is this? Vinyl?" He rubbed his finger against it and decided it was a sort of cloth fabric covered in a sort of waxy, water-repellent substance.

The kitchen, also small, was filled with modern appliances, all incomprehensibly colored the same shade of shit-brown as the club chairs.

The only minor saving grace was the bathroom. Rather large, with a deep, inviting bathtub. Thankfully, everything was white except for a large, pretty, wood-framed, oval mirror that hung above the sink.

He walked back into the living room, and noticed that it also held a small glass-topped dining table with two chairs. The table and chair legs matched; they were made of shiny, ornate brass. Expensive no doubt, but equal in ugliness to the rest of the furnishings.

On the walls, much to his dismay, he saw a number of framed posters; variations of Monet's 'Water Lilies' mostly, and in the bedroom a horrendous print of a cat wearing a beret, sitting in a window of what was apparently a Parisian building.

Who the hell is *this guy?* Peter thought to himself. *Blech.*

He went to the bathroom, splashed some cold water on his face and decided to go for a walk.

After a decade of roaming roughly the same ten dingy blocks in Williamsburg, Peter was overwhelmed by his surroundings. The beautiful, early September weather cradled him gently; he felt hugged by the warmth. He leaned into the thick hot air, pressing his weight into it and imagined that if he let himself go completely it would somehow manage to keep him from falling.

He walked over to the nearby Ile St. Louis, a tiny atoll so charming and entirely unchanged by time that it almost looked like a Baroque Disney village; he half expected the merchants to be dressed in period costume. He spotted a long line of people snaking over the footbridge toward a tiny open window in the front of a café through which something was being handed out. He looked up at the sign, it read: BERTHILLON. They were lined up for ice cream. He tried to imagine what it would be like to crave the taste of something so badly that one would be willing to wait, standing for an hour, in the hot sun, to eat it. He sat on the curb and watched the people for a while. A little girl licked her wrist methodically, lapping up the cocoa-colored drips that had flowed down from her cone; he noticed chocolate specks on the tips of the blonde hairs that had loosed themselves from her messy ponytail. A young couple gave each other a taste of the other's flavor and then openly kissed, their tongues mixing the two tastes into yet a third. Peter looked away.

He got up and walked onward, quickly compelled to take a detour down to the banks of the Seine. He marveled at how accessible it was. In New York City, the rivers, both east and west were foreboding, the city planners, likely afraid of potential lawsuits, had made access to the water near impossible. Iron rails, high piers, had been installed to keep citizens a safe distance from the plumby depths. Here in Paris, one could simply walk down any number of wide, unguarded steps to the water, and so, people did. Everywhere…sitting, lying, their unshod feet dangling mere inches above the lazily flowing Seine. Peter stood on an incline made up of old cobblestones and watched the river lap at his feet, it was like standing on the beach and watching the waves roll in and out, but in the middle of a city.

Pretty, cool, Peter thought to himself.

Seeing Notre Dame in the close distance, he headed over. He looked over his shoulder a few times, sensing that someone was following him. After the third or fourth look back, he cast his eyes downward, it was a cat. Skinny and grey it seemed to be following him. Peter walked backwards a few steps and watched the cat advance toward him delicately, paw over paw, like a fashion model.

Of course. Catwalk. Peter smiled to himself. He loved moments like these, when something so obvious, that one should really have understood before, but somehow didn't, revealed itself.

Finally he found himself standing, looking up at Notre Dame's astounding spires and imagined Quasimodo ringing the bells.

"Ring away, my brother. Ring away! *Vive les freaks!*" he shouted idiotically, his head tilted back, mouth smiling wide in fraternal ecstasy.

His yawp startled a little boy standing next to him, who promptly began to cry.

"I know. I'm scary," Peter said to him, before heading back to the flat, his good mood broken.

On the fourth day, feeling sufficiently acclimated, un-jetlagged and relaxed, he decided to try to eat something. Without hesitation he decided on a pastry. He had been eyeing the beautiful confections closely since his arrival, without any sensation of hunger, but simply as one would covet something pretty. There were three *patisserie* shops within a two-block radius of his apartment. He chose the quaintest, most old-fashioned looking one. The walls were pale peach, lovely cut-glass mirrors hung here and there, and a dazzling display of sweets crowded every case. He looked at every item carefully and finally decided on a chocolate éclair. It wasn't the prettiest of the bunch, kind of turd-shaped actually, but it seemed solid and utilitarian. He deemed it an appropriate first candidate. Shaped like a tube and filled largely with soft cream it should be fairly easy to swallow without much chewing. He speculated that he could eat it with his hands and not attempt a knife and fork, implements that he had not handled in nearly fifteen years. In addition, he had a vague, deeply buried memory, of kind of liking the flavor of chocolate, though he could not remember at all what it tasted like.

"Un éclair au chocolat, s'il vous plait", he surprised himself by asking in decent French.

"Oui, Monsieur. C'est pour emporter?"

He hadn't thought of that. Should he attempt the ingestion here or at home? He glanced around, it wasn't a café per se; it just had a high counter and a few stools for those who couldn't wait until home to eat their treats. Much too precarious for this first attempt, he thought, *Better take it home.*

"Oui, à emporter. Merci."

The lady handed it to him without a bag. The éclair was delicately wrapped in a thin piece of paper, which he assumed was created exclusively for this use since he had never encountered paper of this exact texture before. It was a hybrid of tissue paper, wax paper, and Air Mail writing paper. He placed the pastry gingerly in the palm of his hand, fingers outstretched flat, not wanting to melt it or squeeze it in anyway. He walked home very slowly with the éclair balancing on his open hand; it reminded him of an egg and spoon race at school. The corners of the paper had been twisted shut, but unwound ever so slightly with each of his steps.

Once inside the flat, he placed the éclair on the glass-topped table. He considered a plate, but thought the better of it.

The less fanfare and accoutrements the better, he reasoned.

He opened the wrapping, smoothed it flat and eyed the éclair with interest. It had weathered the block-long trip well, but funnily, it seemed to be sweating a little. Tiny beads of condensation had formed on the top edge of the hard chocolate glaze. It must have been from the change in temperature, but it gave him a reason to break the tension and chuckle.

"That's right, little buddy, I'd be sweating too if I was you!"

It was 4 p.m. Peter sat there preparing to ingest food for the first time since he was twenty-two. He fell into a kind of daze, recalling the initial, dreaded egg and the failed attempt at toast all those years ago. In an effort to prepare his body before the actual attempt, he tried to focus on what the mechanism of chewing and swallowing felt like. Warming up, like an athlete would, he did a dry run and mimicked picking it up, taking a bite, chewing and swallowing. His tongue felt funny in his mouth, he suddenly became afraid he would bite it while trying to eat the éclair. He became agitated, so he walked around the room to calm himself. He sat down again and unintentionally entered a reverie during which all the tastes and textures from his childhood paraded through his brain: pancakes, pop rocks, liver, cheeseburgers, Brussels sprouts, pizza, ice cream; thick, mealy, bitter, gooey, prickly, cold. Anyone watching would have been confounded. An attractive, seemingly sophisticated man, sitting at a table intently facing down an éclair. *Mano a mano,* like gladiators in a ring. It seemed a very uneven match, but astoundingly, the éclair seemed to be winning. The crowd would have gone wild.

A door slammed somewhere in the building's courtyard and broke Peter's daze. He looked up at the clock on the oven, it was 8:07 p.m. He had been locked in battle with the éclair for over four hours. He was furious. He impulsively grabbed it, and swung his hand up to his mouth. It was closed. He willed his brain to send a message to his mouth, to open up, but the wires were somehow crossed, the message didn't get through. He knocked and knocked at the door of his mouth, the éclair smashing repeatedly against his face, to no avail. He stopped. The éclair was now a pulp of brown goo in his fist, and on the edge of his vision when he looked down, he could see blurred bits of slop on his nose and mouth. He was disgusted, defeated.

He eventually got up and washed his face and hands. He was a frustrated wreck. He noticed, while lighting his cigarette, that his hands shook. Deep down, he had really thought that if he put some genuine effort into it, that he would succeed.

"Motherfucker," he said flatly. "Motherfucking fuck."

To steady his nerves and in an effort to comfort himself by doing something he did well, Peter went out into the Paris night in search of a drink.

The hot, humid breeze by the river felt threatening this time, curling around his neck like hands, choking. He pulled distractedly at his collar. He walked up the *quai* and headed toward St. Germain. The streets were filled with people enjoying the last of the summer evenings. The café terraces were packed. Everyone seemed giddy; on the tables, all the beverages appeared to be pink or red hued. He passed by countless bottles of rosé and red wine; the repeated celebratory clink of glass against glass began to irritate him. Suddenly bitter, he was jealous of their levity, their happiness, the camaraderie, the unity.

Normal people, he thought, *doing normal people things, united by normal people goals, how nice for them!*

Paused at a red light, on a particularly narrow street corner, he found himself pressed by the crowd, precariously perched nearly on top of two women sitting around a tiny table. They each held a tall glass filled a very bright scarlet-colored liquid he had never seen before.

Annoyed, he asked aggressively in English, "What the hell is that?"

They looked up at him, startled.

The brunette, pretty and young, pursed her perfect pink lips at him in silent confusion.

"Hey, Amélie Poulain, I'm talking to you!" he added obnoxiously.

Her friend, a curvy blonde, stretched her arm protectively across the petite brunette's chest and answered, "Tango."

"The dance?" Peter was deeply confused now.

"Grenadine *sirop* and beer, idiot American," she said venomously. "Why don't you go back home, back to your land of (she searched in vain for another suitable word)…idiots," she repeated finally in heavily accented English.

Before he could respond the light turned green, and the crowd pushed him onward, their unintentional bumping fueling his anger. His nerves frayed, he just wanted to find a dark, quiet hole to crawl into. But he was now in the heart of St. Michel, the center of university life in Paris. At dinnertime, the smell of cheap food was overwhelming, crêpes, kebabs, Greek food, all available for take-away by the students too poor or impatient to sit at a restaurant table for a meal. Peter was suddenly aware that everyone around him was eating.

"Stop chewing so loud!" Peter yelled. No one paid him any attention. He supposed they were used to 'idiot' Americans.

Again, he was jostled and pushed from all sides, he stopped

briefly to get his bearings but as soon as he had, seemingly out of nowhere, a tall black man, inexplicably wearing gigantic, white fur rabbit ears, said to him in English, "You like jazz?"

"What?" asked Peter, incredulous.

"I said, you like jazz, brother? 20 euro cover and you get some good jazz and a drink."

"Oh, you're a *barker*, go *'woof woof'* at someone else, man. I ain't interested," Peter said rudely.

"I suppose I am indeed a dirty dog, brother, but it's a smooth place and you look like you could use some smoothing."

Peter knew it was a bad idea. It was a tourist trap, but he was swayed by the appeal of sitting in the dark for hours, drinking and not having to make conversation.

"Ok, buddy, what the hell. I'm in."

The club was in a basement and looked just as he had expected; worn-out, red velvet banquettes, low lighting and filled with thick cigarette smoke. A small stage was set up awkwardly in one corner of the room. It was cliché beyond belief, but it was perfect for tonight. Peter chose a small table in the rear of the club; it offered a half-moon shaped bench seat and one chair. He sat on the more comfortable padded bench; this made him face sideways and mostly away from the stage. He would have more privacy like that. Women tended to want to make conversation with him when he was alone in a bar. Often he welcomed it, knowing it could lead to casual sex if he wanted it. Tonight though, he wasn't in the mood.

He ordered a Maker's Mark on the rocks and was told the live music wouldn't start until 10:30 p.m. He settled in, nursed his drink and lost himself in thought.

Suddenly out of nowhere, a nasal, American voice broke his reverie.

"Hi there, my name is Glory. I was named after Gloria, Archie Bunker's daughter on the TV show, you know, *All In The Family* because my mother loved her thick, blonde hair. Do you think if

I had had a brother they would have named him Meathead? I mean, after all, they named my sister Sabrina after the smartest Angel on *Charlie's Angels*, so who knows, right? I've always been pissed about that, I mean, why does she get the smart name?"

Peter looked up slowly. She was very young, maybe twenty-three, a little pudgy, but in that good way that makes young women's breasts bigger and softer. She was short and her blonde hair was cut very close to her head, a sign of rebellion he assumed, but still, she was pretty, though in a completely plain and mundane way.

"I am sorry, do we know each other?" he asked

"No, but the door guy said you were American and that you'd been sitting here alone for hours waiting for the music to start, and he figured you could use some company and I figured we would chat and wait together."

Peter cracked his neck, then his knuckles, paused, and then replied, "I am not waiting for the music to start, I am hiding, but sadly, you have found me, but please go away, I am tired and in no mood to babysit."

Glory's eyes filled with tears. Peter had a momentary pang of remorse; perhaps he had been too harsh.

Before he could say anything else, still standing, not even using the table for support, she erupted into a torrent of words, tears and anger.

"Look you shit sack, you're tired? You're tired?! You smug fuck, I am tired! I just graduated college, majored in archeology, who the hell majors in archeology? What the hell was I thinking? My parents are fucking pissed, I mean what the fuck I am going to do now? I spent the whole summer trying to fucking figure it out while being fucked by European pigs wanting to stick it to a dumb American girl. And then I've got this big load, man, this fucking giant load of shame, it's so fucking heavy sometimes I can't lift my head. At school, you fuck, there was this guy Finn. Finn, how fucking romantic is that? Who names their kid Finn? Too good to be fucking true, man. I should have known: too good to be true. He was gorgeous, he cooked for me, he wrote me poetry, he wrote me songs, but you know what else he did between the meals and the serenades? He beat the shit out me. Every fucking day. For three years my body was a fucking war zone. He was an artist though, the Jackson Pollock of fucking bruises, he'd splatter and splatter his fists on me, but to him it looked like fucking art. I learned to lie like a fucking spy. I hid it from everyone. Everyone. And every day I woke up knowing I should bail. But man, those dorms are like a prison, like a fucking cell sometimes, you know? Dank, narrow, sad. Who can live in that without some hint of splendor? And his hair man, it was this sick, beautiful, beige and brown, like the color of a fucking beach, and his skin man, well he looked like a fucking faun, d'ya know what a faun's skin looks like, you shit? It looks like velvet! It feels like velvet! How do you walk away from that? He's in San Francisco now, probably painting another chick with his fists, creating another fucking masterpiece of fucked-up-ness and I am standing here in front of you, looking for some fucking humanity, but you're tired!" She paused to take a big heaving, snot-filled breath.

He liked her. She was a little overdramatic and over self-aware in that way that college kids are, but she was damaged. He liked damaged people. It must have been her initial perkiness that had put him off. He told her to sit, and ordered her a whiskey. She began to calm down and soon, through her muddy mascara, wordlessly, her eyes told him everything was cool now.

"Here's to getting shit off your chest," she said as they raised their glasses to toast.

By the time the music started, he was barely aware of it. He was very drunk, Glory was very drunk; he had let her ramble on about her summer and contented himself with looking at her breasts and imagining them in his mouth. He wondered what they would taste like, would they taste better than an éclair? Maybe he could spread some éclair on them? Peter sobered up momentarily to better consider that prospect, thinking it might actually be a viable way to successfully ingest food. He sat up straighter in his chair and Glory stopped talking for a minute. He suddenly tuned into the music, the singer was amazing, a woman with a rich, melodious voice, caressing each syllable, stroking each word, she hit the highest highs and low lowest lows with velvet precision. Peter felt himself getting hard. Jesus, what a sordid night this was turning out to be.

He said to Glory, "Wow, that woman really has an amazing voice?"

"What woman?" Glory replied.

Peter turned around in his seat to look at the stage in the distance, in the center of it, fuzzy through the crowd and the smoke, was a small, roundish shape, clothed entirely in black. Peter could not believe his eyes. He got up and walked uncertainly toward the stage, sticking to the shadows on the outer edge of the room. The voice was unmistakably feminine, glorious and full, but the body from which it was emanating was decidedly other. Peter, now just a few feet away from the singer, had to sit down in an empty chair to recover. Right there, in front him, stood the source of the velvet voice, the prompter of his erection: sweaty, redheaded, white-toothed, Dallas Foster.

Peter was transfixed. Dallas stood in the center of the stage, in front of the band, his eyes closed, intently focused on the song he was singing. It was Billie Holiday's *"When Its Sleepy Time Down South"*. He sounded just like her. Not like a man singing her, not like a drag queen doing an impression, but just, exactly, like her. It was eerie.

Take me back there where I belong
How I'd love to be in my mammy's arms

When it's sleepy time down south

He sang beautifully, but more shockingly, it was unmistakably in a woman's voice. Peter looked around; no one else seemed freaked out by it. The place was mostly empty, people were talking amongst themselves more than listening, but still, he couldn't understand how they hadn't noticed. Dallas finished his song, there was a smattering of applause and he walked off the stage toward the bar.

Peter gave him a minute and then approached cautiously.

"Dallas?"

Dallas looked up. Again, briefly, there was that something other in his eyes; a sharpness, and then again it was gone, dissolved into molasses.

"Holy Shit, if it ain't my flying buddy! What the hell was your name again?"

"Peter, Peter Howland… Dallas," Peter faltered. "Dallas, I'm stunned, your voice when you sing, it's…"

"Yeah, freakish I know. It's a little something I discovered by accident singing in church when I was kid. Fat, little, white southern boy, sings like a black girl. Freaks the shit out of most people, so I keep it pretty much under wraps. But I don't know no one 'round these parts, so I figured it was safe to let her rip, but of course, now you're here. Shit, buddy, small world, huh?"

Still stunned, Peter couldn't manage a response; it wasn't just a party trick…no way. It was truly, deeply weird. He knew Dallas was trying to make light of it, but Peter just couldn't move on.

"I mean, Dallas, it's almost otherworldly, I..."

"Aw, buddy, come on, you're boozed up is all, in fact, let's have another, shall we? I am done singing for tonight, so we can get good and lit up together."

Peter certainly could use another drink. He glanced at Glory; she was fast asleep and curled up like a kid on the crescent-shaped seat across the room.

"Sure, let's have a drink," he agreed.

Dallas patted the stool next him, indicating Peter should sit. "So what are you doing here in Paris, my buddy?" Dallas asked.

Peter was momentarily at a loss and then remembered the cover story.

"Writing," he answered.

"Really? Cool. What do you write? Mystery novels? Erotica?" He grinned. "I had a friend once who was a movie reviewer, got to go to flicks for free and write about 'em and get paid – that seemed like a sweet gig to me. Do you do that?"

"No, uh…I guess I write fiction, mostly short stories and some poetry"

"You guess? You don't know what you write? Ever been published?

"Um, yeah, but just in some local literary magazines in New York"

"Well, don't give up, buddy, that's the good thing about being a writer, no expiration date. You can be good even if you've been on ice for a long while."

"What about you, what are you here for?"

Dallas ignored him and went on, "You writing a story about Paris, or a guy in Paris or something?"

"No." Peter reached nervously for a believable answer. "I am kind of exploring the nuances of French cuisine".

Dallas guffawed and patted his round belly, "I'm kind of exploring the nuances of French cuisine myself".

"No, not eating exactly, just kind of exploring what makes food appealing. Why people eat in the first place." Peter was drunk and bluffing and not sure where he was going with this. He noticed his palms getting moist.

"I'll tell ya why people eat, buddy. They eat 'cause if they don't eat, they die! End of story." Dallas smiled. "You were right when you said you wrote short stories, buddy! That sure is a short story!! They don't eat. They die!" Dallas cracked himself up.

Even through the haze of booze, Peter felt humiliated. He had a sudden urge to tell Dallas the truth about himself, just to prove him wrong to wipe that smug look off his face, but suddenly there was a slight commotion at the back of the room. Peter looked over and saw some rowdy American college boys sliding into the seat next to Glory and waking her. He reflexively stood up, feeling protective, what if one of them was Finn?

"Whoa, buddy, chill out," said Dallas, " that little whore can take care of herself."

"She's not a whore, she's a good kid, just a little dramatic and confused, but a good kid. Boyfriend beat the shit out of her for years, she's just a little fucked up."

Dallas started laughing uncontrollably.

"It's not funny, Dallas."

"Um, yes, buddy, actually it is," he managed. "I can't believe you fell for that shit! What the hell? Have you been stuck on the same block for twenty years or something? She's a hooker, my man, a whore. She tells a different sob story every night, drinks for free, goes home with the guy, fucks him, guy feels guilty and is worried about her, gives her some cash to get her back on her feet, and then she starts over the next night."

"No," said Peter firmly. He had always prided himself on being a good judge of character.

"Uh, yes," said Dallas. "You haven't fucked her or given her any money yet though, right? I saved ya in time?"

"Yeah, I guess so." Peter was surprised at how hard this news hit him. He had enjoyed his evening with Glory, two sad sacks wallowing in their shit. Now for the second time tonight, he felt like a fool.

Peter got up and headed toward the bathroom. He did, after all, thankfully, still piss. As he was washing his hands, two of the college boys barreled in.

"Can you believe the tits on that girl? They look like scoops of vanilla ice cream!" one of them said to the other.

"Yeah and that name man, too fucking funny! Glory! Can't believe her old man named her after the American flag! Old Glory! Glory! Glory! Glory!" they chanted in unison, each with one fist pumping the air, the other on their dicks while they peed.

Peter felt the room start to spin. He steadied himself on the hand dryer. The boys pushed roughly past him on their way back to Glory.

Peter was way drunker than he had initially realized and wanted out. He walked from the bathroom straight out the club door without stopping to say goodbye to Dallas.

Outside, the air was cold and damp and it was drizzling a little, but he was happy to be out of the club. He stood there for a minute, looked up at the sky, then looked right and then left, trying to figure out which way was home. He had no idea, but decided to go left. He got about half a block until he heard Dallas' voice behind him.

"Hey, buddy! Where are YOUR manners?! Jeez, I buy ya a drink and you bail without so much as a sayonara? What gives?"

Peter kept walking.

"Oh, I see, I hurt your feelings. Well if it makes you feel any better, I fell for her shit myself, first night I was here. She told me her mother had named her after the morning glory. A beautiful flower, you know, really is. She told me she came over here with her boyfriend and that he had dumped her at a train station in Florence without any money or even her bag. She had left him on the platform waiting for the train, to go get cigarettes. When she got back, he was gone. She looked everywhere. A half hour later, the train came. She had her ticket in the back pocket of her jeans, so she got on it anyway. To Paris."

"Really?" Peter asked. "You're not just saying that to make me feel like less of an idiot?"

"Really, I swear. But I got to tell you, still not sure who lost out the most on this deal, because, Peter, she is an absolutely amazing lay."

Peter felt his knees weaken. He was overtired, drunk, disoriented and in the company of someone that repulsed him and intrigued him at the same time. He was embarrassed for caring what Dallas thought, embarrassed by his own adolescent reactions, everything started to spin, he put his hand on the wall, worried he might collapse. In his mind, Peter floated momentarily above them, like someone leaving their body for that brief instant after death. That bird's-eye view of one's self that believers say is afforded right before heading definitively to heaven or hell. What an odd pair they made, standing in a rainy Paris street in the middle of the night.

"Where are you staying?" Peter asked.

"Don't know yet."

"What do you mean, you don't know yet? You've been here nearly a week."

"I don't like to sleep in the same hotel twice. Weird superstition."

"Jesus, Dallas, you are quite a piece of work," laughed Peter, suddenly amused. "You can crash at my place tonight if you need to." The booze had made him reckless.

Peter thought he'd jump at the chance, but Dallas demurred.

He seemed to sober up and give Peter the once over. "Ok, but no funny stuff. I don't want to wake up tomorrow with a dick in my ass or a knife in my chest."

Peter laughed again, "No funny stuff, I promise."

Unreal, Peter thought to himself. *This freak is afraid of me?*

After a few wrong turns, and ten minutes of failed attempts at punching in the correct entry code – a tiresome technological hurdle necessary in order to enter any residential Paris buildings – they finally made it up to Peter's flat. They were so drunk and tired by then, that they both collapsed immediately and slept in their clothes; Peter on his bed in the bedroom, Dallas on the monstrous teal couch in the living room. It was a welcome outcome; their exhaustion spared them from confronting the usual awkward, personal, bedtime rituals. On the walk home, which was executed in silence, Peter had realized that Dallas had no luggage, just the same black backpack that he had had on the plane.

After only a few hours of sleep, around 9:30 a.m., Peter woke. He was very hung-over and had a hard time getting his bearings. Lying on the bed, in his still damp and smoky clothes, he tried to piece together the evening in his mind. Eventually, he peeked his head into the living room; Dallas was still fast asleep. He went to the bathroom to wash his face and brush his teeth, he considered taking a shower, but felt too vulnerable to disrobe completely with a stranger in the next room. As he cleaned himself up, he realized that he was in fact rather afraid of Dallas. Even after this second meeting, he still knew virtually nothing about him. Peter suddenly felt irresponsible for having let him in.

Peter tiptoed into the living room. Actually tiptoed. It made him stifle a laugh, he felt like Elmer Fudd. Dallas seemed completely guileless. He was lying on his back, sprawled on the couch, soft underbelly exposed. If he had been a creature in the wild, he would surely have been someone's dinner by now.

The backpack was right near the edge of the couch and Dallas' left foot was resting on it. Peter felt thwarted; he had hoped to surreptitiously get a look inside. Instead, he sat on one of the armchairs across from him and took another look at Dallas. He was looking for clues. As usual, Dallas was wearing his black uniform. Generic long-sleeved button-down shirt, black belt, black jeans, plain, black boots. Peter tried to discern if the clothes were expensive or cheap, but he couldn't tell, he knew a true *fashionista* would be able to, but without reading the labels, to him, black was just black. Dallas didn't wear a watch or any other jewelry so Peter had no way at all to gauge his guest. Dallas

Foster could have been a millionaire or a bum.

Peter woke to the sound of running water. He had fallen asleep again in the armchair. Dallas was no longer on the couch. Peter headed toward the bathroom, the door was wide open but he hesitated.

This is my place, damn it! he reasoned, and walked in.

Dallas was in the tub, enjoying a steaming, frothy, bubble bath. His head was tilted back and a wet washcloth was draped over his face. *Well, I guess he's not afraid of me,* Peter thought to himself.

"Comfortable?" Peter said sarcastically, rather peeved at the liberty that had been taken.

Dallas didn't flinch, he just gently pulled the washcloth off his face, which was red from the heat and looked sleepy.

"Oh, hey buddy, hope you don't mind, stole the bubbles from my last hotel, they kinda relax me, I have a real bitch of a hangover this morning, just trying to steam her out."

"I'll make some coffee," Peter said diplomatically. He was afraid to start anything.

Dallas stayed in the tub for another half hour. Peter pouted and felt surprisingly lonely as he waited alone with his coffee in the kitchen.

Dallas finally emerged, back in uniform, but with his hair still wet and neatly slicked back. Like most redheads he had ruddy cheeks and no sign of facial hair. He looked suddenly very young. Peter felt a paternal pang.

"Are those yesterday's clothes? You don't have your luggage with you, wanna borr…"

"Nope, clean set," Dallas interrupted. "I like to travel light. Just the one backpack, but I do have two of everything. If I can wash 'em I do, if not, I just toss 'em and buy another set."

"That's an interesting approach."

"Yeah, makes life easier, plus I was told black is slimming," Dallas said laughing and sucking in his big gut. "Speaking of which, I am starving. Got anything to eat?"

Peter's heart sank, "Um no," he answered nervously. "Haven't really had a chance to stock up yet."

"Well, let's head out then. I'll buy ya breakfast, least I can do after you put me up last night and all."

"Um, I'm not really hungry, but thank you."

"How can you not be hungry? Your stomach must be crying for food after all that booze! C'mon let's go, don't be polite, I can spring for the meal. Let's go."

"Uh, yeah I guess I am a little nauseous from last night, but, I uh…" Peter stammered pathetically. "I guess I could join you for a cup of good French coffee. This stuff I made is frankly awful."

So out they went, Dallas lugging his big pack. Peter had let him take it, not yet ready to address whether Dallas would be allowed back in the flat or not. They chose a café nearby with a lovely view of the Seine. It was another gloriously sunny day and they were lucky to get an outside table. Dallas ordered a ham and cheese omelet with fries and then, still hungry, he had a croissant. Peter sipped his coffee and watched enviously. Eating seemed to come so easily to Dallas, it was almost obscene for him to be sitting with Peter. He ate with obvious enjoyment and abandon, clearly not the least bit concerned about his manners or his weight.

They didn't talk much, just mostly enjoyed the view. An impossibly large weeping willow, planted on the street above the riverbank seemed to enjoy the moment as much as they did. Its long, spineless branches dangled all the way forward as if hunched to better reach the grayish currents. They had grown so long that in the breeze, the tips of the furthest most leaves seemed to absently strum the water, like fingers across piano keys.

Midway through the meal, Dallas simply remarked, "Sure beats airplane food."

The check came, Dallas paid and Peter suddenly felt

awkward. His mind raced, *What next? Is this the end of the road? For crying out loud, we're total strangers!*

If Peter let Dallas crash at the apartment, he reasoned, he would surely soon be curious about Peter's eating habits. Plus, Peter agonized, *What if this guy is a grifter or something? What is he doing in Paris? What is he doing for money?*

They sat in silence a few more minutes and then Peter, gathering his courage, driven by a mix of unsatisfied curiosity and loneliness, decided to take one last stab at getting some personal information out of Dallas. He dove in, head first, feeling he had nothing to lose.

"So, Dallas, what are you really doing in Paris? You seem pretty nimble at dodging the question," he asked.

Dallas looked at him flatly, took a beat and responded, "So, Peter, what are you really doing in Paris? You seem pretty nimble at dodging the question."

Peter was confused and off balance for a second, Dallas had so exactly mimicked Peter's words that it almost felt like weird déjà vu or something.

"I told you, I am here to write," he recovered.

"I don't think so," said Dallas, now looking directly at Peter. The smile in his eyes was gone and the steeliness that Peter had glimpsed before had taken its place.

"What do you mean?"

"That was not a truthful answer. You were clearly reaching. Have you ever even written at all?"

"Yes," Peter answered, a little afraid.

"I believe you," Dallas said flatly.

They sat in silence looking out at the river.

"I mean, you don't seem to have a job here, what are you doing for money?" Peter valiantly tried again.

"I mean you don't seem to have a job here, what are you doing for money?" Dallas countered.

Peter was annoyed.

"Dallas, stop the childish games, I am just trying to get to know you."

"Really? Well then, seems like we are at an impasse, huh? You have no interest in telling me why you are here or how you are supporting yourself, and I also have no interest in telling you why I am here and how I am supporting myself."

Peter thought it over. It was true. Why should Dallas be forced to answer those questions if he himself was unwilling to? Despite his annoyance, "Fair enough," he conceded.

"Look, buddy," said Dallas, the usual soft gleam suddenly back again. "Let's just say we're two guys who like privacy. Why does every acquaintance have to begin with an inquisition? Why are we always forced to decide how we feel about someone based on their background, their profession, their goals? Why can't one just take things at face value? Seems like maybe you don't know anyone in Paris, seems like maybe I don't either, seems like we're sorta getting along, how 'bout we just hang out until we're sick of each other. Just pass the days, you know."

Peter sat in silence thinking it over; he was rather unnerved by Dallas' habit of switching back and forth unpredictably from rube to philosopher.

"Let's go for a walk," Dallas said diplomatically after a while, patting Peter on the shoulder. "It's a beautiful day."

They walked for the rest of the afternoon. Paris has a way of making one do that. The architecture and beauty of the city are so overwhelming that you just keep putting one foot in front of the other, never wanting it to end. They walked from the Left Bank into the Right, through the Marais, and then to Les Halles. In the midst of the chaos of souvenir shops, cheap clothing vendors, American chains like McDonald's and Starbucks, Dallas said, "Shame what happened to this place."

"What do you mean?" Peter asked.

"Well, you know, it used be Paris' central market, back in the day. It was filled with amazing food stalls; they used to call it the 'stomach of Paris'. But as the world modernized, and humanity increasingly craved the antiseptic, the people voted the market out of the city center to its outskirts. They were bothered by the stench of all that food, I guess. Revolted, even."

Peter looked at Dallas, wide-eyed.

"What?" Dallas asked.

"Nothing," Peter replied

They walked on, Peter imagining rotting fruit and offal piled in the gutters.

Soon they cut over to the Rue de Rivoli and wandered under its arcades.

"I have always wanted to go to Buenos Aires," Dallas said at one point. Peter assumed there was a connection to be made, but he was too embarrassed by his ignorance to ask.

They wandered into the Louvre courtyards, stood for a while in front of the I.M. Pei glass pyramids.

"Fucking *DaVinci Code,* sure ruined that," Peter said, finally relaxing a little.

"No shit!" Dallas agreed, laughing.

They pushed forward through the Tuileries Gardens, Peter made a move to sit on one of the green metal chairs by one of the famous *basins* where the tiny sailboats raced.

"No, let's keep walking," Dallas said quickly.

"Just for a minute," Peter answered.

Dallas reluctantly complied.

They both leaned back in their chairs and turned their faces to be warmed by the late afternoon sun. Someone was mowing one of the many meticulously manicured lawns. Peter sneezed from the freshly cut grass.

"I'm getting sunburned," Dallas said after a while. "Redheads and the sun don't mix," he added getting up.

They crossed over the Pont Royal and headed left down the Boulevard St. Germain. Neither spoke, yet it was clear that they were enjoying each other's company. Near Odeon, Peter suddenly realized that they had made a loop and were heading back toward his flat. He spent a few blocks wordlessly wondering which of them was leading. The walk had seemed aimless, but now he questioned if he had subconsciously led them there, or if conversely it was Dallas that had.

He glanced at his watch. It was 6:15 p.m. He was suddenly exhausted.

"Got a date?" Dallas asked, finally breaking the silence.

"No, I was just wondering what time it was. I haven't walked this much in…well I honestly don't think I have ever walked this much."

"Yeah, I know, this city is amazing that way."

"Have you ever been here before?" Peter asked innocently, genuinely interested, not trying to be provocative or to get information.

Dallas seemed to sense that and answered, "Yes. Once, when I was a teenager, on a school trip."

Peter laughed, "Funny, I was here in high school too. Maybe we were here at the same time that time too."

"Ah, a romantic," said Dallas.

"What do you mean?" Peter asked sharply, suddenly defensive.

"Just that you believe in fate and all that shit."

Peter couldn't argue that.

As they neared his street, Peter got increasingly nervous. He knew the decision would be his to make. Would he invite Dallas to stay over? His anxiety was indeed fading and he was admittedly rather intrigued by him. In fact, he had spent much of the walk internally theorizing about what Dallas was hiding. To keep the fear at bay, Peter held onto the idea that if they ever did decide to share their secrets with one another, Peter's would surely beat Dallas' hands down. He hoped it would give him the upper hand in whatever confrontation might arise.

But Peter wasn't ready to share and if he allowed Dallas to crash with him, by morning his lack of food intake would undoubtedly be questioned. He decided to buy time.

"So, Dallas, I am wiped out, I am going to go upstairs and take a nap. But let me give you the phone number to the apartment. I mean, I don't know how long you are here for, but call me if you want to get a drink sometime," Peter said awkwardly. It suddenly felt like he was asking Dallas out on a date.

Dallas didn't say anything for a second, so Peter added quickly, "I'm not gay."

It made Dallas laugh. "I know that, buddy, neither am I. Sounds good. I'll wander around and find a hotel that seems welcoming."

Peter took a small pad and pen out of his pocket.

"Ah, ever the writer, always ready," Dallas said as Peter wrote the number down.

Peter handed Dallas the number. They stood there for a minute and then Peter thrust his hand out. They shook. "See ya, buddy," Dallas said. Then he turned suddenly and headed toward the rue Mouffetard. Peter watched him walk away, a black-clad blob, easily melting into the Paris crowd.

Five days passed without a call from Dallas. Peter was paralyzed. He had not tried food again, he been too distracted. The first day, he figured Dallas didn't want to freak him out by calling too soon. The second day, he wondered if he had offended him and did not leave home at all, afraid to miss the call. The third day, he wondered if maybe Dallas had lost the number, so he took to repeatedly wandering around the block and over to the café where they had had breakfast in the hopes of finding him. On the fourth day, he thought maybe Dallas had left Paris, so he swallowed his pride and went to the jazz bar. No sign of Dallas. On the way out, he asked the bouncer if he had seen the fat, redheaded American guy that sang like a woman. The bouncer looked at him as if he was insane. On the morning of day five, he could not get out of bed.

He was completely perplexed by his feelings. Why was he experiencing such infatuation? It had to be the mystery, he concluded. He hated not knowing the end of a story. It was like having a great movie burnout before the end of the last reel. Peter suddenly understood why the kids back in Brooklyn had been so taken with him all those years; he had been an enigma. In Dallas, he had found a man that was perhaps as inscrutable as he was. He was being given a little of his own medicine. He didn't like the taste.

At 11:47 a.m. on day five, the phone rang. Peter picked up.

"D'ya miss me?" It was Dallas.

Peter didn't know how to respond, Dallas was kidding of course, but the truth was Peter had missed him. Terribly. He got a grip of himself and decided to play tough. "Who is this?"

Dallas laughed, "It's Dallas, you jerk, d'ya know lots of folks in Paris with a southern drawl?"

"Oh hi, Dallas, what's up?"

"Well, Peter," Dallas continued in a false formal voice to match Peter's faux indifference. "Just checking in to see if ya wanna grab some grub with me tonight. I found an amazing, cheap cous-cous place in the Marais."

"Sorry, can't do dinner tonight, but how about we meet for a drink afterwards?"

"Okay, your loss. I'm telling ya, it's great fucking cous. Okay, so let's just meet back in St. Germain. There's a bar that I like there off rue du Four, called Chez René, it's easy to find, meet you there at 10 p.m.?

"Fine, see you then."

"I'll be the one stinking of spicy sausage!" Dallas guffawed before hanging up.

Peter decided to get there a little early and have a drink to loosen up a bit and drain off some of the nervous tension of the last few days. The place was a rat hole: miniscule, filthy, and saddled with a gag-inducing combination smell of cheap wine and vomit that hit him in the face at the front door like a one-two punch. Why Dallas liked this place, he couldn't imagine. Jammed between the sweaty patrons, perched on a rickety, too-high stool at the bar, he 'accidentally' plowed through four Maker's Mark on the rocks in a half hour. By the time Dallas finally barreled in, he was already pretty hammered.

"Hey ya, buddy!" Dallas shouted. Peter stood up to greet him and accidentally knocked over his stool. "Whoa there, told ya you should have had some dinner first."

Peter ignored him. "How was your dinner?"

"It was good, actually took that kid Glory with me, she needed a good hot meal."

Peter was astounded. He felt betrayed, by both of them.

"Was it a date?" he sneered.

"No, Peter, she's a fucked-up whore. I just feel sorry for her. Wanted her to have one night where she didn't have to associate fucking with food."

"Where did you find her?"

"At the club, she's there pretty much every night. I've been singing there all week, so I kept running into her."

Peter sat quietly. He didn't know what to say. He didn't want to let Dallas know he had gone looking for him, but he was annoyed. Was Dallas lying? Was the bouncer lying? Dallas certainly hadn't been there when Peter went the other night. Neither had Glory. He had looked for her too.

Dallas ordered himself a beer and got another round of bourbon for Peter. They talked a little about Paris history, French music and politics. Each one carefully and subtly sidestepping any personal questions, careful not to divulge very much about themselves. At this point it was almost becoming a game. Who would tell less? Who would crack first?

At about 1 a.m., the booze got to Peter and as usual, he needed some air.

"Let's head outside," he said to Dallas. "I need a breather".

"I know a bakery a few blocks away, they bake the morning bread this time of night. They know me now, we can grab ourselves some loaves, fresh out of the oven. It'll help sober you up."

Peter shook his head and started to respond, but Dallas insisted, "I know, I know, you're not hungry, but it'll do ya good."

Peter, too drunk to argue, too numb to panic, did not protest.

The bar was on a side street and the sidewalk was very narrow. Dallas walked out first, ahead of Peter, to lead the way. He took one long step out the door and into the street, skipping the sidewalk entirely. As Peter breached the doorway, he saw Dallas fly up into the air, very high, about ten feet, like he was a soaring bird. Peter thought it was a trick at first, because he appeared so graceful. Later he would realize that he had instantly gone into the kind of profound shock that makes everything seem to unravel in slow motion. A blur of white zoomed by under Dallas as he was up there floating in the air; but it was gone, having screeched around the corner by the time Dallas hit the ground right at Peter's feet. The car had been going so fast that it had not projected Dallas forward, but simply flipped him high up in the air and down, back onto the same spot; like a seal flipping a rubber ball on its nose.

The street was now completely deserted and quiet, the speeding car had somehow wiped away all traces of humanity, as effortlessly as an eraser wiping a messy board, clean. Dallas lay there immobile, not in a tangled heap as one would expect, but reclining on his side, as if asleep. Peter was afraid to even breathe, as if a simple exhale, a minor change in air temperature, a whisper, might accidentally blow the man laying on the ground in front him, towards his death.

Just as Peter started to notice blood oozing from Dallas' head, a rush of people came pouring out of the bar. Peter just had enough time to note the poetic synergy of the two events before he was pushed out of the way by the crowd. A woman screamed and hid her face in the shoulder of a man standing in front of her. An old man in a shabby coat, hovered over Dallas until an ambulance arrived. He looked over his shoulder and said to no one in particular, "J'ai vu ça pendant la guerre."

Surprisingly quickly, an ambulance arrived, barely managing to squeeze itself down the small street. While the medics worked on Dallas, Peter focused on the siren's tinny sound, "*pin- pon, pin-pon,*" it wailed over and over. It sounded French.

Peter, having been shuffled involuntarily to the outer edge of the gawking semi-circle, could barely see Dallas at all as they loaded him into the vehicle. Before his brain had a chance to react, Dallas was whisked away. Rooted in place, he watched the ambulance pull away, slowly at first and then faster, until it just disappeared. Peter blinked. The crowd dispersed unexpectedly fast, and within fifteen minutes, it was if nothing had happened on the little street. But Peter could not move. He just stood there, a soft breeze swirling around him, lulling. A while later, Peter couldn't be sure how long, the bartender came out to have a smoke. He noticed Peter standing there immobile. He walked over and touched his arm surprisingly gently.

"Salpêtrière," he said.

"Huh?" Peter managed.

"Hôpital…Salpêtrière."

Peter nodded.

He forced himself to move, his limbs felt heavy. He walked slowly up the street a little toward the main boulevard, vaguely beginning to formulate the thought of finding a taxi. Up ahead of him, on the edge of his left field of vision, something caught his eye. Half in the gutter, straps hanging down like little legs, almost as if it was sitting patiently on the curb waiting to be rescued, was Dallas' backpack.

Peter walked slowly toward it. Instead of picking it up, he sat down next to it. After wanting so badly to know its contents, under the circumstances, it felt almost disrespectful to pry. He and the bag sat there in silence for a little while. It felt familiar, almost like he was hanging out with Dallas. Then impulsively, Peter violently unzipped the main compartment. He undid the zipper all the way around in one quick gesture and everything came pouring out into the street. The bag was filled with lots of little boxes of different sizes. Peter picked one up and read the label, then another, and read that label, and so on. No severed heads, no dead animals, nothing creepy after all. Dallas' bag was simply filled with tooth whiteners. Every possible permutation; pastes, strips, gels, they were all there; a seemingly endless assortment of brands and options. Peter checked the rest of the bag's pockets and apart from a spare set of Dallas' uniform (black shirt, black pants, black socks) that's all there was. It didn't explain much, but it did explain Dallas' exceptionally white teeth.

On the boulevard, Peter cut to the front of the taxi line. There always seemed to be a line for taxis in Paris, even in the middle of the night. "Emergency," he muttered, over and over as he pushed past the people waiting for a ride home, most of them were too tipsy to protest.

A cab finally pulled up and as he leaned in the window to tell the driver where he was going, a young man in line angrily shoved him forward and Peter hit his head on the car door. He knew a small gash had opened at the base of his hairline but he just calmly repeated what he had been told to the driver,

"Hôpital Salpêtrière."

The man's girlfriend, upon hearing Peter's destination, pulled on her boyfriend's sleeve in an effort to calm him. To save face, he still yelled some intelligible insult at Peter's departing taxi.

Peter touched his brow and looked at his fingers, in the darkness they looked as if they had been dipped in maple syrup. He licked them clean and pulled a lock of his thick hair over the cut.

Once at the hospital, he had no idea where to go, so he walked in through the emergency bay, and went up the nurse's station. She was in her fifties and very heavily made-up. It startled him. Nurses were supposed be clean, neutral-looking, virtuous. She looked like an aging whore. She was a little overweight and had huge breasts, which were jammed suggestively into her too-tight uniform. Her perfume was very strong. *This wouldn't be allowed in America,* Peter thought to himself. *There ought to be international rules.*

He asked her if she spoke English. She smiled suggestively, implying that indeed she did.

Peter put on his 'all-business' voice and said, "A friend of mine was brought in about an hour ago, hit-and-run victim, a man named Dallas Foster."

She checked her computer.

"I am sorry, I have no one of that name."

Peter felt a rush of panic as the enormity of what had happened suddenly caught up with him.

"Um." He hesitated, almost afraid to even ask the question. "If the person that was brought in did not survive, would they still be listed in the computer?"

"Yes, sir," she said and looked up at him, the flirtatiousness ebbing and with kindness filling her eyes.

"Perhaps, he did not have any ID on him," Peter offered. "He is a white male, a bit overweight, reddish hair, in his early thirties, maybe late twenties."

The nurse clickety-clacked on the computer some more. "I am so sorry, sir. No one matching that description has been brought in tonight."

Peter paused, his hands gripping the cold, steel counter, Dallas' heavy backpack hanging on his right shoulder painfully. He looked down at her nametag, it read: MATHILDE MASSELIN.

"Mathilde!" he said out loud.

"Oui,"she replied, startled.

He searched to find the original lines of her face under the thick make-up, unrealistically hoping to find the Mathilde of his childhood beneath the layers of artifice. He badly needed his beloved nanny tonight. He also found a fleeting suggestion of his mother in the face before him, and he suddenly missed her very much.

He thanked her and walked out the emergency doors into the street to have a smoke and to think about what to do next. "Maybe it's the wrong hospital?" he said to himself, rummaging in his pockets for his cigarettes. In the darkness, he heard the click of a lighter and the unmistakable smell of tobacco. Over to his right, were the medics that had worked on Dallas. Lit by the ambulance's headlights, they were leaning against it, smoking.

It *was* the right hospital. Just as Peter was about to approach them, he heard the nurse's voice behind him.

"Monsieur! Monsieur!" she shouted from the door. Peter walked back toward her.

"You did say it was a gentleman you were looking for, yes?" she asked.

"Yes, why?"

"Well, because there was a female matching that description brought in tonight."

"No, no, thanks for trying. He's a friend of mine, definitely a man," Peter laughed and patted her arm. He turned to go try talking to the medics.

He took one step forward and froze. Billie Holiday.

Peter's legs involuntarily buckled underneath him and he fell to the ground. The medics rushed towards him. They helped him up and back into the hospital, where they sat him in a hard plastic chair, Mathilde gave him some water.

His mind was racing, replaying every moment since his first meeting with Dallas, but he could make no sense of it, it all rushed past his brain in scattered, kaleidoscopic bits. He was sweating.

Mathilde sat down next to him and looked at him questioningly.

"This woman, you think perhaps it is the man you are looking for?" she asked, seemingly unperturbed by the absurdity of her question.

"Yes, I think it might be," Peter somehow managed.

"I will get the *docteur* to come speak with you," she offered.

Peter sat numbly and waited. His mind was blank. The doctor appeared after what seemed like an eternity. Thankfully, he spoke English too. It should have been a huge comfort, but it made Peter feel guilty for being American.

"Hello, sir, I am Dr. Vareille, I treated your friend." Peter stood up. "Because you are not family I am not supposed to share information with you. However, since we do not have any contact information for them and because your friend is in such critical condition, I will make an exception." Peter sat down.

"She has suffered extreme trauma to the head, but thankfully her skull was not cracked entirely open, only fractured. Her shoulder and right side took the most of the impact. She has a broken collarbone and arm, three broken ribs and fractured tibia. Because we were able to stop the internal bleeding quickly, if the brain swelling goes down as we hope it will, we feel that she might pull through."

Peter sat silently. The doctor gave him a chance to absorb the information; he was a pro.

Peter finally looked up at the doctor and asked, "Are you sure she is a woman?" It was the doctor's turn to sit. Of all the questions he had anticipated, this certainly was not one of them.

"What do you mean?" he asked Peter, thinking his English was failing him.

"Just what I said. Are you sure this patient is a woman?"

"I am not sure I understand."

"Okay, Doctor, I am going to be frank, I met your patient a few weeks ago, he introduced himself to me as 'Dallas Foster', that's a man's name in America," Peter continued, pushing past a fleeting moment of panic as he realized that it was actually a genderless name. "And during all of our, repeated interactions, he has behaved as, and led me to believe that, he was a man."

The doctor looked very confused. "Perhaps we are not speaking of the same person. My patient's name is Claire Anderson. She had in her jacket, a wallet with a California driver's license. I assisted on Miss Anderson's operation and I can tell you that she is without a doubt, a woman."

"May I see the driver's license?"

"Sir, I fear I have already shared too much, as you are not family. I am sure you understand."

Peter gave him a pleading look. Lucky for Peter, it was now nearly 3 a.m. and the end of a long shift for Dr. Vareille, lucky also that he had worked fifteen monotonous years in the ER, dealing mostly with household accidents like cuts and burns. Sure, he'd heard his share of crazy stories, but nothing like this, and luckiest of all, he was nosy by nature. Peter's questions had more than piqued his curiosity. He went to get the wallet.

In the few minutes it took the doctor to return, Peter felt his first sense of calm. Claire Anderson from California, there had clearly been a mistake. This wasn't Dallas after all. He must have been taken to a different hospital and this poor, overweight woman just happened to have been hit that night as well.

He heard the doctor's footsteps down the hall. He had the

wallet in his hand and had already pulled the license out for Peter. Peter decided to stay seated for this one. The doctor handed it to him. Peter looked at it. It was Dallas. Unmistakably. With the photo cropped as it was, he did in fact, look like a woman. He also of course, still looked like Dallas. There was a certain androgyny there that Peter had never noticed before. Minus the body language, the booming southern drawl, the masculine swagger and endless sexual innuendo, Dallas did actually pass as a woman. An overweight, unfeminine woman; but a woman none-the-less.

Peter's eyes scanned down. Claire Anderson, 5′8″, 204 lbs. Eyes – green, Hair – red.

5436 Fountain Avenue. Los Angeles, CA 90048.

Suddenly it was all too much for him and he vomited involuntarily. Of course there was no food to expel, only a bit of bourbon and bile.

"I am so sorry," he said to the doctor.

"You're in shock," the doctor replied calmly.

"You can say that again."

"I think it's best if you go home to rest, it's been an emotional night for you. Leave a number with the nurse, we'll call you if there's any change. If not, stop by tomorrow during visiting hours."

Peter allowed a cab to be called for him. He went back to the apartment, put Dallas' backpack on the teal couch and looked at it. He then placed it on its side, as if it were lying down, he leaned over and kissed it gently.

"What the hell am I doing?" he asked himself. "My God."

He walked into the bedroom and lay down fully clothed on the waxy mustard bedspread and fell asleep immediately. He did not dream.

The next morning, still lying on his back, Peter opened his eyes but did not move. He was too afraid to set the day in motion. Dallas had lied about everything. Not just his gender but his provenance too, he had never said anything about Los Angeles. Peter wondered just how much of Dallas was a lie. He felt humiliated, betrayed. Vulnerable. Was the accent a sham too?

Peter could not bring himself to think about Dallas in female terms, though the evidence was irrefutable. To him Dallas was still a drunken, southern guy. He couldn't really imagine him any other way. His mind raced. Peter visualized how Dallas had gorged himself on food; suddenly the hearty eating seemed forced. It was obvious now; Dallas simply ate to keep weight on to camouflage his breasts. Was he just a run-of-the-mill transvestite? Or was he fleeing something? The law? Peter forced himself to get up. He needed answers. He took a shower and looked at himself in the mirror.

"Suddenly not so smug. Suddenly not so unique," he said to his reflection.

When he got to the hospital it was 3:30 p.m. Peter hoped he had not missed visiting hours. A different nurse was on duty. She was young and scrubbed, he fleetingly wondered if the new international rules had been issued overnight. He approached the desk.

"I am here to see one of your patients," Peter said in French. For some reason today, he felt like fitting in.

"Name please," the nurse asked innocently.

Peter hesitated, it all seemed so surreal, "Claire Anderson".

After a few minutes of back and forth about the fact that he was not family, Peter recounted the previous night's events and was finally allowed to enter the bowels of the hospital and proceed to the nurse's station in the intensive care unit.

The first question the ICU nurse asked him was, "Are you the husband of Miss Anderson?"

Peter felt a wave of heat crash over him and he began to sweat. "No, just a close friend," he replied wiping away a lock of hair that had just begun to stick to his forehead.

"Well, she is doing miraculously well. Her injuries were major, but there is no brain damage. She will need an enormous amount of rest, but she was conscious for a few hours this morning. I'll let you in, but will allow you to stay only fifteen minutes. It's for her own wellbeing, I am sure you understand."

Peter nodded and silently followed the nurse into the room. Dallas was lying on his back. His head was heavily bandaged and he had a black eye and swollen lip. His right leg was hoisted up in traction, in what seemed to be a ridiculously uncomfortable position. In the genderless hospital gown, Dallas still looked very much like Dallas.

Peter went to sit in a chair next to the bed. He wanted Dallas to wake up. He leaned in to whisper his name and suddenly wondered what he should call him. Dallas or Claire? Peter decided on Dallas.

"Dallas," he tried. "Dallas, it's Peter, how are you feeling, buddy? You ok?"

Nothing.

"Dallas, I brought your backpack. All your shit is safe, wake up, buddy."

Nothing.

"Claire...Claire...wake up, honey," Peter whispered. Dallas's eyelids fluttered.

Peter felt a funny feeling in his stomach.

"Claire, sweetie, you're okay," Peter said in a paternal voice. Dallas opened his eyes.

They were unfocused and dull. He seemed to be straining to see. It was heartbreaking, now wasn't the time for confrontation, Peter switched back, "Dallas, buddy, over here, it's me Peter."

Dallas shifted his eyes to the right where Peter was sitting. First nothing, then recognition, Dallas started to moan and squirm. Peter tried to calm him.

"It's okay, buddy, calm down, you were in an accident but you are going to be okay, buddy, just calm down."

Dallas closed his eyes.

"Buddy, say something. Are you okay?"

"Wow, them French cars is made of tougher tin than they get credit for, huh?" Dallas said in a hoarse whisper.

Peter was fascinated. Had he had not been conscious of having been called 'Claire'? Or was he just so manipulative that even in this fractured state, he had found the strength to continue the charade.

"Aw, buddy, great to hear your voice," Peter chose to simply reply.

Dallas closed his eyes again. The nurse came in and asked Peter to leave. The patient needed to rest, she explained.

"Patience with the patient," Peter said under his breath as he left the room.

For the next week, Peter's life revolved around Dallas. He visited the hospital every day. When not there, he read, walked around, went to a few movies, saw a few art exhibitions, but everything was just killing time until he was allowed back to the hospital.

Dallas had told Dr. Vareille that he did not wish to contact his family in the U.S. and had given a formal okay for Peter to visit as often as he liked. But whether out of concern for Dallas or out of selfishness, the nurses kept his allotted visiting time to a minimum. Peter therefore, spent most of his hours in the hospital hovering around the nurse's station, flirting with them. Sometimes he'd escape to the cafeteria. He was fascinated by the hospital food. The colors were duller and blander than food he saw in restaurants, the shapes also seemed more uniform. He wondered if there was a difference in taste. Despite his inquisitiveness, he opted not to give it a try.

Back in the ICU, the nurses were intent on getting Dallas to eat, saying it was crucial to his speedy recovery. But he was still in a lot of pain and doped up on meds, and still not hungry at all. To keep him alive, he was instead fed nutrients through an IV drip. For that long week, Dallas and Peter were unintentional brothers in arms – both were alive, neither were eating.

Dallas drifted in and out of consciousness, waking only for a few minutes a day to offer Peter a sarcastic southern bon mot. Peter often sat in the room and watched Dallas sleep. He also watched the effects of food deprivation slowly take shape on Dallas' body. He was losing weight, rapidly. Day by day, Peter noticed his features thinning out. Soon he had a neck and eventually, even his arms lost their thick, ham-like appearance. By the end of week two, when the doctor declared Dallas well enough to be moved out of the ICU, he must have been at least twenty pounds lighter than when he was brought in.

That first day out of intensive care was a big milestone in Dallas' recovery; a threshold had been crossed. Peter arrived to find him sitting up in bed watching French TV. His leg was still elevated on a heap of pillows, but it was out of traction and all the bruises on his face finally had healed, leaving only a slight yellow tinge around his right eye. From the way the door was angled, Peter could see Dallas before Dallas saw him. He marveled at his transformation. His short, red hair, combed by the nurses, was styled in a distinctly feminine fashion. He of course had no make up on, but the weight loss had made him much less masculine, he now had an almost ethereal, vulnerable quality about him.

Peter made a little shuffling noise to announce his arrival and walked in. Dallas shifted and pulled the bed sheets up to his chin. Peter knew he was concealing his breasts, which must be more pronounced now that the fat that had previously surrounded them had melted away.

"Wow, buddy," Peter said. "You look much better today, big turnaround, huh? How are ya feeling?"

"Much better thanks," Dallas replied in a low voice "...but I'm just not hungry; at all. Sometimes I feel like I'll never be hungry again but the nurses say they won't release me until I start eating solid food. They bring in the food, I look at it, mush it around on the plate, they cajole me for like an hour, but it's like I am blocked, I just can't put it in my mouth. Weird, huh? Being that I used to be such a porker and all."

Peter did not respond.

"I am losing tons of weight," Dallas continued, "and it's freaking them out, they keep telling me I'll die if I don't start eating soon. Trying to scare me straight, I guess."

"You should eat," was all that Peter could manage to say.

"Yeah, thanks, buddy, no kidding. You have no idea what it's like, I just can't make my brain understand, and I have absolutely no taste for anything. Doctors say it could be from my head trauma. Hopefully, it'll pass."

Peter gripped the arms of the chair he was sitting in to steady himself. The room was spinning. A door seem to fly open in the back of his brain, it felt like a rush of water, he realized it must be euphoria. He had finally found a twin soul. But then he quickly remembered that much as he wanted it to be, this wasn't really true, because instead of sustaining, Dallas was wasting away.

"You okay, buddy?" Dallas asked of Peter, reversing their roles for an instant.

"Yeah, sorry, its just so good to see you feeling better."

Dallas' eyes shined. For the first time, Peter noticed they were a pretty green.

"Well, I'd better rest up," Dallas said quietly. "Thanks for coming by"

Peter got up. "Dallas, I'm not going to be able to stop by for a few days, my parents are in town," Peter lied. "But I'll be back soon as I can. The nurses have the number at the flat if you need anything."

"Okay, buddy, no worries, I'll be okay. Have fun with the 'rents."

"Eat something, will ya," he tossed at Dallas on his way out. Though it was the last thing he wanted, it seemed like the appropriate thing to say.

Peter had lied because that morning, halfway through a conversation with Malabar, his *gardienne*'s Yorkshire Terrier, with whom he had routinely taken up chatting with in his building's courtyard, he had realized that he needed a break. With no anchors other than Dallas in Paris, he was starting to wonder if he had lost his mind. Was this all really happening, or was it simply a figment of his imagination. It was so preposterous, all of it. How could it possibly be true? He needed a reality check. He called his mother.

"Hi, Mom".

"What's happened?"

"Nothing, Mom, maybe I just miss you?"

"Come on."

"Mom, it's just that I got close to this guy here and he had a bad accident, and I've spent the last three weeks in and out of the hospital and I'm just a little depressed.

"My God, you're gay."

"Jesus, Mom, no. I just wanted to hear your voice."

"Well that's a first."

"I'm okay now, Mom. Thanks. Talk to you later."

Peter hung up the phone and screamed, "WHAT NOW?!" at the top of his lungs.

Peter took a full five days off from Dallas. He tried to move on and establish a new routine. He'd go to the patisserie every day and choose a new pastry and attempt to eat it. Like a wrestler tackling a slew of increasingly colorful opponents he valiantly tried to defeat each one, in vain. They always won. They remained uneaten. Dallas was all he could think about. It completely freaked him out. In an attempt to push him out of his mind, Peter thought about all of the women he had slept with over the years, dissecting each one in intimate detail, each mole, every wrinkle, the way they smelled, the texture of their hair. One morning, while he was contemplating if 11 a.m. was too early for whiskey, the hospital called.

"Mr. Howland?"

"Yes."

"This is Dr. Vareille."

"Is everything okay?" Peter asked, alarmed.

"Yes, Mr. Howland. In fact, we feel that Miss Anderson has sufficiently recovered to be released from the hospital, but we do not feel she can manage alone, and as you know, she knows no one other than you in Paris."

"Has he eaten?"

Again, the doctor doubted his English, "No, *she*, has not, but we feel that perhaps if she is moved into a domestic scenario, the block will lift, and that the reestablishment of normal habits will trigger her appetite."

"Are you saying, he wants to come stay with me?"

"Well, we haven't discussed this with Miss Anderson yet. I felt it was better to be sure you would be available. We did not want to upset her if you were not. The pins will remain in her leg for another month, so she will need help with most things, like walking, dressing and bathing. We can arrange for home care for the bathing if you are uncomfortable with that aspect, but she will really just need someone around to help her manage all things in the short term."

Peter sat up straighter. The time had come. He would finally have an opportunity to get the answers he wanted so badly.

"That should be fine, but, Doctor, please allow me to come in and discuss this proposal with *her* myself."

"Fine, Mr. Howland. À demain."

Peter arrived at the hospital the next day with unusually steady nerves. Despite everything that lay ahead of him, he felt oddly calm.

Once again, standing in the doorway of Dallas' room, Peter could not believe his eyes. Dallas had lost still more weight, the color was back in his cheeks, and his small features – pug nose, tiny pink lips and rounded button chin, that had previously given him a porcine appearance, now made him look almost pretty.

"How are ya, buddy? Sorry, it's been so long."

"Okay, I guess. I feel way better but kinda weak. They are pumping me with protein and energy liquids, but I still ain't my old self."

That's the understatement of the year, Peter thought to himself. "Yeah, that's why I am here, Dallas. They want you to try life on the outside, to see if your appetite comes back. But they can't release you on your own recognizance, so I thought you could hide out at my place for a while." Peter had no idea why he was employing prison lingo to facilitate this difficult conversation.

Dallas closed his eyes. He said nothing for about fifteen minutes. Peter paced the room like a hungry wolf.

Yeah, buddy, one hell of a decision ain't it? Peter thought smugly to himself.

Peter finally guessed what the sticking point was, so he offered. "Of course, I'm no nurse, so they'd have a professional come to bathe you and stuff, I wouldn't want to be responsible for breaking that leg of yours again."

"I don't have that kind of money, Peter."

Impulsively Peter answered, "I do. I'll take care of everything, we can figure out the finances later." Peter hoped he hadn't divulged just how badly he wanted Dallas to say yes.

After another long silence Dallas answered, "Well, I suppose I have no choice."

"Good, it's settled then. I'll talk to the powers that be and I'll come get you tomorrow."

The next day, in an effort to keep Dallas from panicking and changing his mind, Peter arranged to wait for him in a taxi outside the emergency bay. He hoped this would allow Dallas some privacy when saying his thanks and goodbyes, and to spare him the fear of being called Miss Anderson in Peter's presence. Of course, deep down, as Dallas signed his bill and his release papers, all in the name of Claire Anderson, Peter imagined that he must have had an inkling that the cat was out of the proverbial bag.

From his position leaning against the cab, Peter watched Dallas emerge from the hospital. It was the first time he had seen him dressed since the accident. He was back in his black uniform. Because of the enormous weight loss, the clothes now hung loosely off his body. The folds of the fabric serving to camouflage his gender the way the layers of fat had before. To all those who did not know better, Dallas' secret would have remained intact. Per hospital regulations he was in a wheelchair and to get him into the cab, Peter had to lift him. He felt very light and small. There was a brief, unspoken moment of mutual tenderness as Dallas hung awkwardly in Peter's arms.

On the ride back to Peter's flat, Dallas didn't say a word, but just looked out the window at the Paris streets.

The first day passed without incident. Peter settled Dallas into the bed and he slept all afternoon and into the next morning. Peter slept on the dreaded teal couch, but poked his head into the bedroom at regular intervals like a nervous father. It was Dallas who ended up waking before Peter on the morning of the second day. From his position on the couch, Peter woke to a series of stage whispers.

"Peter, Peter. Are you awake? Peter?" Dallas whispered loudly from the other room. Still too weak to maneuver on his own, he needed Peter to get out of bed.

"I need to pee," were Dallas' first words of greeting.

"Good morning to you too, buddy," Peter laughed.

"Sorry, I just really have to go, all these liquids they are pumping me with are killer on the bladder."

Peter helped Dallas into the bathroom; when they reached the toilet, Dallas hesitated.

"I know its kind of a pussy move, but I am a little wobbly, I think I'd better sit."

Nice save, Peter thought to himself. "Sure, buddy, no worries." Peter sat him down and left the room. "Call me when you're done."

A few minutes later, Dallas called for Peter and asked to be set up on the couch in the living room for a change of scenery. Once he was all cozy and set, he turned to Peter and said, "Well, I guess first order of business is that I'd better try and eat something, that's why I am here, right? What's for breakfast?"

"Oh wow, buddy, I am such an idiot, I've got nothing in the house, I'll run out and get something, what do you want?"

"Gosh, you know the deal is I really have no taste for anything, that's the problem, I haven't eaten in so long I kinda don't remember what anything tastes like. I guess I'll just have what you usually have."

Peter's brain raced and finally came up with the suggestion to head to the nearest patisserie and bring back whatever looked good.

Once on the street Peter felt woozy. How would he manage to keep up the charade? He walked around the block a few times before heading to the patisserie. When he got there his eye was immediately drawn to his old nemesis…the éclair.

"Fuck it," he said to himself. "He and I can try to beat that shit-shaped little bastard together."

This time he decided on coffee éclairs, instead of chocolate; somehow less threatening and definitely more breakfast-y.

Back at the flat, Peter produced the éclairs.

"Eclairs!" Dallas laughed. "For breakfast?!"

"Well, they are coffee-flavored," Peter smiled. "And I figured they'd be easy to eat and a good place to start."

Peter got two plates and placed one éclair on each. He helped Dallas to the kitchen table and they both sat there silently facing down their enemies.

"God, this is so weird," Dallas said. "Before the accident I was such a hog, I'd have eaten this thing right out of your hand when you walked in. Now, it just seems like such an insurmountable feat."

"I know how you feel," Peter replied.

They sat there for a few minutes staring at their plates.

"You go first," Dallas finally said.

"No, buddy, come on, this is important for your recovery, just focus. You can do it."

Dallas smiled at Peter, picked up the éclair, sniffed it, licked at the edge where the hole to put the cream in was oozing a bit and then took a little bite.

He chewed slowly, seemingly letting the little bit of cream and pastry find its way all around his mouth, as if reintroducing his taste buds to an old friend.

His eyes gleamed and he opened his mouth and finished the rest of the éclair in two swift bites. "Well. I guess I am cured. Must have been the shock and some weird reaction to that crappy hospital food. Yee haw! Dallas is back!" he yelled, pumping his fist in the air.

As if there were reprising roles from their very first meeting on the plane, Dallas wordlessly reached over and ate Peter's éclair.

"Hope you don't mind, buddy, I haven't eaten in weeks and you eat all the time."

He had had high hopes for this tandem ingestion attempt. This unexpected outcome was devastating, but Dallas's glee was so infectious that Peter laughed despite himself.

His appetite now back in full working order, Dallas drew up a grocery list for Peter. Peter could not believe his predicament and like a brave solider heading out to battle, he put on his coat and headed out to the grocery store for the first time in fifteen years.

He didn't know where the local market was so he had to ask a stranger for directions. Once inside, he did a first walk through to steady his nerves. Then, after feeling sufficiently confident that he could blend in, he mimicked the other shoppers and got himself a grocery cart. He wheeled it awkwardly down the aisles and started looking for items on the list. He was overwhelmed by the choices. Dallas had asked for seemingly innocuous items like cereal, jam, cookies and tuna; but of course, in each category, the market offered countless options. Peter was paralyzed by the diversity. Finally, he ended up just randomly grabbing items, usually based on the brightest packaging or the prominence of their display. By the time he exited, he was sweating profusely.

"Jeez, sure took you long enough," Dallas shot at him when he finally returned.

"Crowded," Peter mumbled as he unpacked the bags.

Dallas surveyed the purchases eagerly from his perch on the couch.

"Did you lose the list?" he asked.

"It was packed in there, I am not good with crowds, I'm sorry, I just kinda grabbed whatever I could get my hands on. Hope it's okay."

"Sure, hell, haven't eaten in so long, it'll be good to eat anything."

Dallas ate some Lucky Charms and a box of chocolate cookies. "I can't believe they have Lucky Charms in Paris," Dallas commented as he wolfed down the food.

Once he was finished, he dozed off again. It seemed as if he had been too focused on himself to notice that Peter hadn't eaten anything.

Peter sat in the armchair across from the couch and watched Dallas sleep. *What are you?* Peter thought to himself.

Dallas was curled into a ball this time, protectively perhaps, and was snoring slightly. With Peter's long black coat draped over him, his skin, in contrast, looked almost chalk white. Peter spent the next few hours working up the courage to face the inevitable. Today, he finally decided, would be the day to confront him.

Her.

About three hours later, Peter decided to wake Dallas, but not before he had gotten up and washed his face and combed his hair. He wanted to look his best; after all, he did have a woman in his apartment.

"Claire," Peter said gently. "Wake up."

Dallas shifted. "Claire, wake up, or you won't be able to sleep tonight."

Dallas opened his eyes; he seemed unperturbed.

Dallas yawned and stretched a little. "Wow, was I out long?" he asked Peter.

"You were asleep for about three hours, Claire."

Dallas' eyes sparkled. "What did you call me?"

"I called you Claire, that's your name isn't it? Claire Anderson?"

Dallas remained motionless, but his eyes sharpened on Peter. "What are you doing?" he asked.

"What do you mean? I am calling you by your name, Claire. Would you like a glass of water or something?"

Dallas didn't respond. Peter was impatient, suddenly overeager to get on with it. He knew this wasn't the best way, that it was too rough and kind of mean, but he didn't care, he wanted it all out. Now.

"Dallas Foster doesn't exist. You are a woman, from L.A. no less, and your name is Claire Anderson. Now that you are feeling well enough, I would like to know, why you lied to me, how long you have been living as a man and why you are in Paris."

Peter felt a burst of adrenaline. He suddenly understood why some people were so power hungry. For the first time in his life, he felt in complete control, he held all the cards. It was a rush.

Dallas seemed surprisingly controlled. He asked Peter to help him swing his legs down so he could sit up properly and face him. Peter smugly settled back into his chair and waited to hear what he was sure would be an extraordinary story.

"Peter," Dallas began, "why did you stop eating?" The southern accent was gone.

Peter was taken aback by both the question and the voice that had formulated it.

"What do you mean?"

"Well, Peter, seems to me you never eat. Ever. Why did you stop?"

Even though Dallas was turning the tables on him, Peter felt oddly calm. "Well, I guess one day, I just got tired of it."

"Well, that's also why I stopped being a woman."

Peter laughed despite himself. "It's not that simple."

"Yes, it is. You stopped eating on a dime, that's a big decision too. You could have died. We all can make big decisions at the drop of a hat."

Peter stayed silent for a while. Deep down he was scared.

"How do you know I never eat? Perhaps I just don't eat in front of you."

"Actually, it was just a guess, but based on your reaction, clearly, it was a good one."

Peter felt his anger rising.

"But you just can't decide one day to stop being a woman. You're a woman!!!"

"Well then, right back at you, you can't just stop eating one day. You're a human being!!" Dallas paused for a moment and then went on. "You stopped ingesting food and somehow, your body adjusted, you survived. Same thing happened to me, one day I had enough of the world from one perspective and decided to make a change. My body adjusted, I survived. It was surprisingly easy. The day I met you on the plane, was my second day as a man." Dallas paused for breath. "How long have you known about me?"

"Since the accident, the hospital. They had your ID. They told me."

"I figured you might know. Were you freaked out?"

"Of course I was freaked out, Dallas. What the hell do you think?"

"I know. I was pretty believable as a man. It's amazing how little people pay attention, even at the ticket counter, when the agent looked at my passport and ticket, she still wished me a good flight, 'sir'. I think the big personality and the drawl were a good choice. They distracted people from the details."

"I'd say so. Did you like being a man?"

"More than anything I liked being someone else, I'm sad it's over."

"It doesn't have to be. I won't share your secret if you don't share mine."

"When did you stop eating?"

"In a diner in Brooklyn. I was repulsed by an undercooked egg and just stopped."

"Yes, but when was that?"

Peter looked Dallas straight in the eyes, "About fifteen years ago."

"Wow."

Dallas and Peter stared at each other wordlessly for a long while. The doorbell rang. It was the nurse coming for bath time.

"I'll go for a walk. Leave you two alone," Peter mumbled as he walked out the door.

Dallas was still lying. Peter knew it down to his core. Underneath the steely stare, the steady voice, the flippant matter-of-factness, Dallas was still hiding something. Peter had watched a hot red cluster of irregular splotches rise up through Dallas's paper-thin, translucent skin. On his chest, and neck, just where his black shirt was opened a button. He had seen those types of splotches before. On his mother's chest and neck as she struggled to retain a semblance of outer calm while a storm of emotion raged within her. He lit a cigarette and chuckled, imagining Dallas in the bath thinking about what Peter had just revealed. The casualness of his reaction belied his incredulity. Dallas didn't believe Peter either.

Nothing had changed.

He walked around for about two and a half hours, trying to clear his head. On his way home, he stopped at the newsstand and bought Dallas a stack of women's fashion magazines. He had always had a good sense of humor.

When he got back to the apartment, he could tell from the quiet that the nurse was gone. He also had a strong sense that Dallas was gone too. He was right. Claire had definitively taken his place and was sitting at the kitchen table with his back to Peter, writing something.

"What are you writing?" he asked.

"An IOU," Claire replied just as Peter rounded the table to face her. She had make-up on, mascara, some powder that evened her ruddy complexion, crimson lipstick, small green dangly earrings that matched her eyes and a simple but lovely, long-sleeved, black-cotton dress. Her hair was slicked off her face in a stylish manner. She looked very pretty. The transformation was finally complete. It was startling.

"Well I guess you won't be needing these," he said, tossing the magazines on the kitchen counter. He leaned against it casually, but it was to steady himself.

"Ha. Ha," she replied, smiling up at him. "Well, I have never been this thin my life, thought I'd may as well take advantage of it and embrace the femininity."

"Good job," Peter said, still taking her in. "What's the IOU for?"

"All the money you laid for the hospital bills and for the extra cash I gave the nurse to go out and buy all this stuff for me. I took it out of the kitchen drawer. You put it there when you came back from grocery shopping, don't you have a wallet?"

Peter sat down at the table across from her.

"I have a wallet," he said neutrally and went on. "Claire, Dallas is gone?"

"Yes, he is; for now anyway. Doesn't the red lipstick make my teeth look really white?"

Peter laughed, "Yes it does."

"I have always been very vain about my teeth. Even when my body let me down, they were always there for me; straight, strong and white. I take very good care of them, they are my best feature."

"Not anymore," Peter leered, staring at her breasts.

"Peter, are you hitting on me?"

Peter had to admit. Insane as it was, he was attracted to her.

"Oh Jesus, Claire, I don't know. I mean…could this get any weirder?"

"Yes, it could actually. But I'm flattered. I wasn't exactly a man magnet before. Peter, have you ever been married?"

"What the hell kind of question is that?"

"Well, have you?"

"No."

"Why not? You're very handsome."

Peter didn't know what to say.

"No eating. No long-term nookie?" she offered. "I'm serious."

"Me too." Then Peter suddenly realized that if he appeared to open up a little more, maybe Claire would too. "I guess I was always afraid that if I shared my secret, the woman in question would think I was crazy, or a freak or something. Whatever, either way, she'd leave me. So I always left first. Less painful that way, I suppose."

"I'm still here."

"Yeah, but you don't count, you're hardly someone I would ever want to be married to," he said flippantly.

There was a flat silence. He had hurt her feelings. He found that interesting.

"Why, because I am arguably even more fucked up than you?" she finally asked.

"No, we're pretty even on that front."

Claire just sat there, thinking it over. "Why then?" she asked again.

"Dallas, I mean, Claire…well there you have it!! I still see you as a man. How can you seriously ask me that? There's your answer."

More silence.

"The nurse left me crutches. Let's go out and eat something," she said brightly.

"Claire, that's not funny. You know I can't."

"Why not? It's easy, I bounced right back, didn't I?"

"But for me it's been fifteen years."

"Peter, stop exaggerating."

"I'm not exaggerating, Claire."

"Peter, I like you. Don't be a typical man and feel like you have to one-up me, to be more mysterious than I am. It's no big deal. Just be yourself."

"Claire, I don't know what to tell you. I am being myself. Actually, oddly, I'm being myself for the first time in my adult life."

"Okay. I just don't see how it's possible, but I am willing to play along. You have been really, really good to me, Peter," she said seemingly sincerely. "I owe you that. Maybe more."

They sat in silence again.

"What now?" she finally asked.

"What do you mean?"

"Well, can I still stay here?"

Peter felt that rush of power again. He let the silence gain some weight before answering.

"You can stay."

She smiled.

"Until you heal up," he added.

She stuck his tongue out at him.

For the next two weeks, they settled into a fairly mundane domestic arrangement. Claire slept in Peter's bed and Peter on the couch. They woke at separate times, they read, they did the crossword out of the *Herald Tribune*, Peter went for walks and sometimes helped Claire to the park nearby where she could sit on a bench and get some air. Like a long-married couple, now disappointed and bitter at how the other had turned out, they lived a life of somewhat wary, mildly antagonistic, companionship.

Peter had gotten better with the groceries and did the shopping so Claire could cook for herself at home. She put on some weight, plumped up a bit, but she didn't turn back into Dallas. The few extra pounds just served to put color back in her cheeks, and much to Peter's dismay only made her more voluptuous. They stuck to neutral subjects so as not to pry too much into each other's pasts; Peter wondered if Claire would ask about the food again. But she didn't. She would just cook for herself and never ask Peter if he wanted anything. Peter assumed that Claire just thought that he was eating when she was asleep, or while out on one of his walks.

Eventually Peter realized that all these years he had worried somewhat needlessly; women didn't give a shit how much of a freak you were as long as you paid the bills.

A month or so into their odd arrangement, they got a phone call from the hospital. It was time for the pins to come out of Claire's leg. They were removed, and after a few weeks additional of physical therapy, Claire was walking unassisted again, but she was left with a slight limp that she would keep for the rest of her life.

Peter watched her walk around the apartment one morning,

"You're good as new. It's amazing."

"I am better than new," she replied, her eyes filling with tears.

"Oh Christ, Claire, don't get all *Lifetime Television* on me, now."

"I am serious, Peter, sick as it sounds, I have never been happier in my life."

"Why is that sick?"

"Come on."

"No really, why?"

"Um, well…I am living with a man that I met when I was pretending to be a man, I had a car accident that nearly killed me. Said man, does not eat yet is somehow radiantly healthy. Frankly, Peter, sometimes I think I died that night outside the bar and that this is all…not real."

"Funny, I felt that way at the hospital when I found out you were a woman."

"Really? Do you think we were both killed?"

"Claire, come on, of course not!"

"Well, how do you know?"

"I called my mother."

Claire laughed, "And?"

"Trust me, we're alive."

Peter got up to go to the sink for some water.

"Make love to me," Claire said flatly.

"Are you nuts?"

"Come on, I know you want to," she paused. "I've seen you look at me."

"Claire, this is crazy. You know you're still Dallas to me somehow."

"Just go in the bedroom and wait for me."

"Claire, stop it."

"Please," she said firmly.

Despite himself, Peter felt himself wanting her.

"Go in, close the door and just wait for me."

Peter did as he was told. He went into the bedroom and closed the door. There was no place else to sit, so he sat on the bed. What seemed like a long while later, he heard a little knock at the door.

"You ready?" Claire asked.

Peter didn't know how to respond, but after a beat, the door opened anyway. Claire was standing in the doorway completely naked. Her body was round and her breasts were large and full. He was immediately aroused.

She shifted a little and Peter noticed that her skin was shimmering.

"If you won't make love to me, I want you to try eating me."

Peter was horrified. "What the hell are you saying?"

"It's honey. I covered myself in honey. It's not really food, but it's a start."

Peter thought back to that night with Glory, how he had imagined her breasts covered in éclair. Maybe this wasn't such a bad idea after all.

Claire moved toward the bed and lay down. Peter just sat there, transfixed.

"Lick me," she said.

"Claire, this is getting gross."

"Peter, you are a grown man, you've had sex before. Lick me."

Peter picked up her arm; it was sticky in his hand.

"Claire, I can't. I just can't."

"It's not food, Peter, just pretend my skin is really sweet."

He looked at her arm again and then at all of her body. Lying down, her breasts had spread like fresh dough. Her skin was very white under the amber honey and she looked like a cinnamon bun.

Peter sniffed her like he had all the items he had tried to eat since OVO, and then he took a leap of faith and licked her. The sweetness shocked him, coursed through him, like a junky's first hit of heroin. He licked her again and again. While she moaned and wriggled, he licked and licked. He could not bring himself to actually have sex with her but she came, and he came. And once she was clean and white again, they lay there silently. She hadn't really been made love to and he hadn't really eaten.

After a while, they faced each other. Propped up on opposing arms, faces only inches apart, they unintentionally began to breathe in unison. Peter licked his lips, which had become dry, and captured a final taste of honey, his tongue darting out and back swiftly, like a snake's.

2

Claire had never noticed that Peter's eyes had flecks of yellow in them. They had always seemed a rather boring shade of blue. Now, as he stared back at her, Claire saw halos of ochre petals, radiating in perfect circles around each of his pupils.

Just like sunflowers, she thought dreamily.

The arm on which he had propped his head to look at her, must have started to prickle with pins and needles. He rolled over onto his belly, turning his head sideways, breaking the spell.

A lock of his longish, soot-colored hair was curled, almost like a question mark on his forehead; she brushed it gently away with her hand.

She got up and walked to the bathroom. Her skin crackled slightly with each step; Peter's saliva mixed with hint of honey.

Before stepping into the shower, she paused to look at herself in the mirror above the sink. It was long and oval and because of her height, she could see herself all the way down to her upper thighs. She smiled reflexively. Never in all of her life had she looked like this. She was still perhaps a little overweight by today's absurd standards, but she felt full and feminine. She ran her hands down her sides slowly, hourglass perfection; in her mind she heard a low, slow whistle.

She was particularly pleased with her breasts, which had, for most of her life been nothing but another roll of fat; shapeless and horizontally elongated like dough rolled lengthwise. She cupped them in her hands and thought they now looked like large, cherry-topped cream pies. No wonder Peter wanted them in his mouth.

In the shower, she let the almost scalding water turn her skin red; she was used to pain, and hardly felt the heat. When she got out and faced the mirror again, she looked as if someone has splattered dark magenta paint all over her.

"I am a masterpiece," she said admiringly.

She slicked her red hair back away from her face. It was just barely long enough to tuck behind her ears into a short, copper-colored bob. She gave it an extra tug as if willing it to grow faster. With just a few magic strokes and a series of intimate licks, after years of closing herself to the possibility, Peter had restored her will to be woman, and now it felt as if the journey back couldn't happen fast enough.

She walked back into the bedroom where Peter had fallen asleep. He shifted position onto his side and hugged a pillow. She allowed herself to hope that he had reached out for her mid-slumber. She gently touched the pillow, as if it were somehow a piece of herself.

She slipped on her black dress and picked up the tiny, green plastic earrings the nurse had so thoughtfully picked out for her. She had been so moved at the attention paid. She wondered if Peter knew what color her eyes were.

She felt around her lobe for the tiny hole she knew was there somewhere. One afternoon at the age of twelve, bored and frustrated in a way only suburban children can understand, she had decided to pierce her own ears. She knew some measure of precaution should be taken: an ice cube for numbing, a potato to place behind her ear to catch the force of the needle, perhaps? But in the end, she had simply taken a needle and thread (the thick, waxy kind used for beading) out of her mother's sewing kit and calmly pushed the needle through her right lobe and pulled the black line all the way through as if darning a sock; and then done the same on the left. She had let the pieces of thread hang like upside down 'U's through her lobes for a minute or two, before tying each into a tiny knot. She remembered having stared at herself in the mirror for a long time afterwards, beads of blood on each lobe, shimmering like rubies.

"What are you up to?" Peter said, startling her.

"Just thinking," she answered, turning and walking towards the bed.

"Wow, Claire. You look all glow-y. Really very, very

beautiful."

Still lying on his stomach, Peter arched his neck up at her like a cobra. He rolled over and she saw that he had a hard on.

"Apparently," she giggled, her eyes travelling to his crotch.

"Ugh, sorry." He rolled over again.

"No, don't. I'm flattered."

She leaned over him and kissed him. She gently slipped her tongue into his mouth and undid his jeans at the same time. He didn't resist. She pulled his penis free, hiked up her dress and sat on him in one seemingly seamless motion. They sucked in their breath in unison, as if equally surprised by the circumstance.

"You're not wearing any underwear."

"I just got out of the shower."

"Your skin is still hot." He pretended to burn his hand on her thigh.

She slid her pelvis up and down in a few long, slow motions. He came immediately. She let out a laugh.

"I'm sorry, it's just that you feel so good. Claire, you smell like vanilla. Is that possible or am I losing it?"

"It must be the body lotion the nurse bought," she said sniffing her own arm. "Mmmm, it *is* yummy."

She gently disengaged herself and lay on her back.

She looked at Peter. "'EAT ME', said the cake to Alice."

"What?"

"Nothing."

"*Alice in Wonderland*, Claire? Seriously?"

"Don't make fun of me."

"I'm not. It's just, all this romance and whimsy, it's quite a departure from Dallas."

"Well, what can I say? I can relate. She's too small, then she's too big. Everything's always just out of reach either way."

"What's just out of reach, Claire?"

"Everything. Nothing. Whatever. I'm tired."

"Ok." Peter exhaled, rising to go to his usual sleeping spot on the living room couch.

"No. Stay."

"Do you really think that's such a good idea?"

"We just made love, Peter."

"No, we just had sex, Claire."

"Wow, even in extraordinary circumstances, men never forget how to be total assholes. The depth of their innate douche-ness is almost impressive actually."

"I'm sorry. It's just all very confusing. Claire seriously, remember, not long ago in my mind you were a man. A rather repulsive one at that, now you wanna cuddle? Christ, give me some time to adjust."

"Fine," Claire snapped. She turned away from him and closed her eyes.

"Well you've certainly had a speedy adjustment back to womanhood. Talk about innate douche-ness." He walked out of the bedroom and closed the door hard, stopping it just short of a slam.

The next morning Claire woke up first. Her arm was draped across her eyes in an unconscious effort to block out the sun. She had fallen asleep without closing the shutters. There must have been a little leftover scent of vanilla lotion in the crook of her elbow that made her wake up hungry and craving pancakes. She opened the door slowly. Peter was still asleep. He had changed into some dark grey sweatpants and a t-shirt. She stood over him and looked at the shirt. Peter was lying on his side; the large, white, block letters tumbled together so that the only ones she could decipher were: B R O K N.

"Broken!" she covered her mouth to stifle a laugh.

She sat in the armchair across from him.

"Ouch," she whispered reaching underneath her. She had sat

on his pants, the belt buckle digging into her butt. She yanked the pants away, annoyed. His wallet fell out. She picked it up and held it in her hand delicately, like a wounded bird. This tenderness surprised her. Perhaps it was because she actually knew almost nothing about Peter that holding this small private object felt like she was holding his heart.

The wallet was dark brown leather and very worn. Like most men's wallets it had vaguely shaped itself to the curve of Peter's ass. She smelled it. She turned it around in her hands and rubbed it with her thumb as one does a stone in a pocket on a beach walk, absently yet rhythmically.

Inside were the usual items; some cash, credit cards, a driver's license. In the small square photo, Peter's hair was cut very short, his ears stuck out slightly, they were back-lit for some reason so that the tips appeared translucent.

She stuck her fingers in the last little leather slit, the one that doesn't show the edges of cards, the secret one, where boys usually keep condoms. In it, she found a photograph of a handsome young man in tennis whites, long legs, holding a wood racket and smiling broadly at the camera. He looked a lot like Peter.

"That's my dad," said Peter from his reclining position on the couch across from her. "When he was young," he continued, sitting up, the word B R O O K L Y N revealing itself across his chest.

"Peter, I'm sorry, I..."

"Claire, it's fine, it's human nature to snoop. It's beyond our capacity to resist that temptation. Really, it's okay."

Still, she looked away, embarrassed. "Why this picture?"

"He nearly died of throat cancer eight years ago. Now, he speaks through one of those freakish little contraptions that you hold up to your voice box. It's deeply disturbing. He was always such a talker, a ham, he got rich off his gift for gab; he could sell sand in the desert. There's something about that picture that moves me…the youth, the hope, the beauty, but it also depresses me terribly, the sadness and darkness of how things turned out for him. I dunno, I can't really explain it, the duality of it speaks to me, I guess; fabulous and horrific all at once. That's life in a nutshell isn't it?"

"Yes."

They stared at each other in silence, the picture still in Claire's left hand, the wallet in her right.

"I want pancakes," Claire finally exclaimed.

Peter laughed.

"Let's go find some."

"Claire, you know I…"

"Oh, Peter, for fuck's sake, when will you stop this act?"

She realized her words were like a punch. He exhaled and let his shoulders drop forward.

"I thought you understood, Claire. It's not an 'act'. I can't talk about this again. Really, I just can't."

"Fine. Will you come with me and at least have a coffee? I read about this place in the paper called Breakfast in America, it's in the Latin Quarter, it's supposed to be just like home."

Peter stared at the floor.

"C'mon! We'll pretend we're at a diner in Brooklyn!"

He looked up at her, eyes wide in surprise and said flatly, "Fuck you, Claire."

She turned, startled. Then she realized.

"Oh no, I'm so sorry. I didn't mean to be sarcastic, I was just…"

"I think a day apart will do us some good. You go, I'll see you tonight."

Claire didn't protest. She showered, and headed out without another word. Once on the street, she burst into tears. She was devastated. *I don't know how to do this. I'll never be able to do this. How do women do this?* Her mind rambled, leaping frantically from thought to thought.

She had closed down her heart years ago, closed it tight, like a small ship trying to make it through a raging storm, battened down the hatches, tightened everything up, gone down to emergency rations, closed her fists tight, switched the light to dim and waited, not for a man, but for death. Until Peter, she had been immune to hope.

She very much wanted to walk the entire way to the restaurant, it had always cleared her head, but she knew she wouldn't make it. The limp tired her out too much, too quickly. She took the metro a few stops and contented herself in walking the last few blocks along the Seine.

Once in the 'diner' she looked at the menu. It kept its promise and offered pancakes, waffles, all sorts of edible Americana.

The waiter came to take her order. He was American, part of the authentic experience.

"Two poached eggs, please," she said gripping the slimy plastic menu a little too tightly. "Make 'em a bit runny, okay?"

While she waited, she dug her thumbnail into the paper tablecloth making a haphazard series of moon-like semi-circles.

"Will I gag?" she wondered.

"How were the pancakes?" Peter asked as she walked in the door around 6 p.m. It was late fall and the night came faster and faster, with her new female form and vulnerable limp, she still wasn't really comfortable being out alone after dark.

"What?" she said, pretending not to hear, but relieved he wasn't still angry.

"The pancakes, Claire, your craving, remember? Did they live up to your expectations?"

The waiter had passed her request along and the kitchen had complied, the whites were mostly translucent and shivered nakedly like clear jellyfish.

He's right. It is revolting, she had thought to herself.

She had punctured each egg with the tip of her fork as she imagined Peter had all those years ago. But she hadn't pushed the plate away, repulsed. Instead she'd smiled. The yellow seeped across the plate like the sun coloring a sky, gold. She dabbed a piece of bread in the mixture and she felt as if she were dipping into the core of something important. The bread was still warm and as she chewed she thought that perhaps she had never tasted anything quite so good.

She had eaten ravenously, so quickly in fact, that a group of teenagers in a booth across the diner stopped their chatter to stare at her briefly.

Done, she had pushed her chair away from the table, arched her back slightly and put her hands on her stomach and patted it.

"Uh…they were good," she finally replied.

"*Good*…that's it? What kind did you have, blueberry?"

"Stop asking me so many questions, Peter!" she snapped, her nerves, shot.

"Yikes. Sorry. What's the big deal? Just curious."

"What do you care? Do you even remember what blueberries taste like? Or pancakes for that matter?"

"Not really. No."

"Then why ask? It's fake sharing, Peter, it's like having a conversation with a deaf guy about the nuances of Jazz. Impossible."

Leave them before they leave you, less painful that way. She was following his advice.

"Well, we're bitchy today. Do you have your period?"

"Oh. My. God," Claire spat, pausing purposefully after each word. "You can't be serious, Peter, did you read a *How-To* book on maximizing your asshole potential this week? Jesus, who are you?"

"Who am I? Dallas Foster? How dare you even go there?

Claire Anderson?" He emphasized the question marks at the end of each name so dramatically that they almost appeared drawn in blood on the living room walls. And then, almost as if an afterthought, under his breath, in a barely audible whisper, one additional word, "Freak."

The sound of the word vibrated in the air like a just rung bell and hung there for a while until it dissipated into silence.

They retreated to opposing corners of the room, like boxers.

Peter lit a cigarette. Claire eventually let herself slide down the wall she was leaning against and sat on the floor. They stayed in their respective positions for the length of Peter's smoke. He absently tossed the cigarette into a half-empty coffee cup and it made a small sizzling sound that instantly reminded him that Claire had asked him not to do that anymore. She had recently taken a sip of his leftover coffee and gotten the booby prize of a butt along with it.

"I'm sorry, I know you hate it wh…"

"I killed my brother," she interrupted.

He blinked.

"I'm sorry, I know you hate it when I do that, I forgot, I'm really sorry. And I'm sorry I called you a freak. I realize how absurd and mean that is. I mean really, if anyone is the freak, it's me."

"I killed my brother."

"Claire, what on earth?"

"When I was twelve I killed my brother. He was thirteen, well almost fourteen."

"Claire, stop it, I hate this kind of crap, really. What are you thinking?!"

"I was a really overweight child, Peter; ruddy, pink-skinned, like a pig. He called me 'Wilbur'. He teased, taunted and terrorized me my entire life." She spoke flatly, as if reciting something long ago learned and repeated too many times so that the feeling in the words was gone. "The morning I got my first period he caught me while I was pulling the sheets off the bed. My mother was still asleep. My father was on the road. '*What happened? Where are you bleeding from?!*' he asked, hysterically. I just stood there, immobile. I guess my quiet made him increasingly agitated. He grabbed me and twisted my arms this way and that, looking them up and down. '*Wilbur!! Tell me!! Where?*'"

She paused and closed her eyes before continuing. "He finally dropped to his knees and inspected my thighs, touching them only with the tips of his fingers as if they were somehow dirty. '*God, you are so fucking fat. Yuck,*' he said disgustedly. Something inside me snapped I think. It was like a dam bursting. In my mind I saw a rush of rust-colored water breaking apart piles of logs. I grabbed his head, and shoved it between my legs. His arms flailed and he struggled to regain traction, but his knees, encased in his flannel pajamas, just slid around on our wood floor. His name was Lance. Lancelot. My mother was kind of a dreamer," she concluded matter-of-factly.

"Well that's a hell of a story," Peter snipped coldly, not believing a word of it.

"It's not a story, Peter. It's the truth," Claire said looking at the palms of her hands, as if hidden there she might find a better script, a more effective way to explain her feelings. But her emotions had faded over the years. Once vivid, they had dulled first to a paler shade and now they disintegrated in her hands like a cotton cloth left too many days in the scorching sun.

"Dallas, Claire, whoever you are. You expect me to believe you suffocated your brother by smothering him in your newly fertile crotch when you were twelve? Come on."

"It's the truth. It's horrible, and when you put it like that, it's even more grotesque, but it's the truth."

"Are you trying to one-up me again, because of my not eating thing?"

"No, Peter, I'm not playing games. I want to know you. Understand you. And I would like for you to know me and understand me. You can't begin to understand me if you don't know this."

"Okay, I'll play ball. Why aren't you in jail?"

"I dragged him down the hall and put him under the sink in my parents' bathroom. Curled him there, like a sleeping cat." She looked away from Peter. "My mom didn't see his body until she already had her underwear around her ankles and was sitting down for her morning pee. He had suffocated somehow, but there wasn't a mark on him. No one ever, even remotely, thought it was me."

"Good God. You are not joking."

"No, I am not joking. It shaped the entire rest of my life."

"I guess!"

"I didn't do it on purpose."

"The way you tell it, it seems as if you did"

"I didn't mean to kill him. In my head, I just needed for him to stop talking. It was an accident."

"How can you recount this so calmly?"

"It was a long time ago. He was a little prick." The pain of his relentless abuse rose up within her. An emotion, found.

"Are you saying he deserved to die?"

"In a way, yes."

"Holy cats. You're God now?"

"No, Peter, are you?" she asked innocently.

"What?"

"Nothing." She looked away, embarrassed.

Peter lit another cigarette and asked after a long beat, "Claire, are you serious?"

"Yes."

She picked at her nails.

"Peter?"

"What?"

"Have you really not eaten at all in over fifteen years?"

The cigarette smoke caught in his lungs like a ghost. He

coughed loudly, nearly choking. Finally he caught his breath.

"Wow. You are one tough chick."

"No. I really just want to know."

He looked her dead in the eyes, "That is correct. I have indeed, not eaten at all in over fifteen years."

Claire pushed herself up from her position on the floor and walked towards the bedroom, she turned in the doorway and looked directly at Peter.

"Freak," she said calmly before closing the door behind her. *Hurt them before they hurt you.*

Despite the events of the previous night, Claire somehow slept well. Yet waking, she felt a buzz of nerves in her stomach and a bitter taste in her mouth that she recognized as adrenaline. As she made the bed, she sang some Billie Holiday; it had always calmed her.

"Southern trees bear strange fruit... Blood on the leaves... Blood at the root..."

Down south, during high school, after her brother's...death, before her father had asked to be transferred to California, she had spent a lot of time in church. She'd often stop in the flat, cross-topped, modern building on her way home from school; she wasn't seeking answers, she was seeking refuge. The kids had a new game; they'd constantly bump into her. Their adolescent implication was she was so fat they couldn't get past her. Though the school halls were wide enough for a row of *Rockettes*, arms linked, to kick through, she found herself propelled like a fleshy pinball though it's circuitous hallways, day in day out. It was exhausting.

The local church was such an ugly building; she paused to marvel at its hideousness every time. She often thought God wasn't even in there because it was such an insult. She'd see her reflection in the big glass doors as she entered, and wondered if God hadn't come into her either because her form was equally injurious to Him.

She'd sit in the nearest pew to the door as if the possibility of having to make a quick escape was always present. The huge wax Christ loomed dramatically over the main altar, incongruously ornate amid the modernity of his surroundings. She liked his crown of thorns the most, and secretly wanted one.

One afternoon, she heard a sandy shuffle of half-sung, half-whispered words, "*Southern trees bear strange fruit… Blood on the leaves… Blood at the root…*" melodically wafting over from a distant, echo-y corner. Claire went to investigate. Kneeling, face turned downward, neck hanging limp as a fading flower, she found a skinny black woman praying to Mary in a small chapel off the main nave.

"The scent of magnolia sweet and fresh… Then the sudden smell of burning flesh"

Claire pulled her jacket tight around her, but the woman must have heard Claire's heart quickening through the down vest (her dead brother's that her mother had ceremoniously given her as if handing over something sacred.)

"That's beautiful," Claire said, but found her voice oddly tight.

"You are fat, girl," the woman said matter-of-factly, before bowing her head again in prayer.

Claire felt a wave of humiliating heat wash over her, the vest suddenly felt oppressive, as if Lance was somehow behind her, his mean macho arms crushing her ribcage. She tried to conjure Peter's delicate touch to counter the frightening memory.

"Here is a strange and bitter croooooooop…" Claire filled her lungs and let the last word quiver loudly as she tucked the last corner of the sheet purposefully under the bed's edge in a concentrated attempt to shatter the thought.

She heard an ironic clapping sound coming from the living

room.

"Hell yeah! Just what I needed; Dallas is back!" she heard Peter shout through the closed door.

Claire pressed her eyes shut, took a deep breath and opened the door.

He was standing directly on the other side and she ran right into him. Like a 'cute meet' in a romantic comedy, they were nose to nose and practically locked in embrace as they awkwardly tried to steady each other.

They looked each other directly in the eyes as if mutually searching for an answer buried deep inside the other one. She pulled away first and walked to the kitchen.

"What the hell are we going to do?" Peter asked her.

"What do you mean?"

"Well, Claire, I'll spare us both yet another recap of our situation, but I think you'll agree it's pretty challenging."

"I guess."

"You guess?!"

She looked away.

"I think I'm in love with you, Claire."

She did a Jimmy Durante style spit-take with the water she had just taken a gulp of.

"Gee thanks, Claire, how romantic."

"Peter, what do you expect? What happened to your '*Eww, you gross me out, you're still Dallas to me*' speech from… YESTERDAY!?"

She didn't believe him. The turnaround had been too quick. She could only see him as yet another predatory male. The hatches were battened again. Her heart, closed. The window of opportunity to sail safely to more temperate shores, lost.

"I don't know. I told you the truth and you're still here. You told me the truth and I'm still here. That's something isn't it? You know? What the fuck? Wanna give it a shot?"

"I'm not in love with you, Peter."

His eyes widened.

"Yes, you are."

"No. I am not."

"Why not?"

"Because."

"That's mature."

"Peter, I appreciate everything you've done for me, you even made me feel like a woman again, but I am not in love with you."

"Claire, newsflash – you are a woman."

"But I never felt like one before."

"Claire, you're what? Thirty-five? You told me the plane was your first day as Dallas, how is it possible that you never felt like a woman before?"

"Because when I look in the mirror I see a pig. Literally." She made a faint oinking sound. "Lance made sure of that. This is the first time in my life I have worn make-up, Peter. Couldn't before."

He rolled his eyes.

"No, I'm serious. I looked in the mirror and saw no nose, no lips or eyelashes. I saw a pig face, a pig snout. For real, as real as if I was wearing one of those latex Halloween animal masks."

"Oh, Claire, come on."

"People stared, I realize now it was probably because I was fat, but at the time, I thought it was because I was pig in pants."

He laughed.

"Really. People would stare at something like that in the supermarket, right?"

What could he answer? It was such an absurd question.

"After the car accident," she continued, "when I was in the hospital losing all that weight, the first time you called me Claire, I heard you. I pretended not to, but I heard you. You were looking down at me so incredulously I sensed you were really seeing me. Me. Of course you were just fading Dallas out and tuning Claire in, but to me you were seeing the woman beneath the pig; the girl beneath the piglet."

She got up and went to the window and looked out.

"You know, it all started because one summer my mother asked Lance to read me *Charlotte's Web* at bedtime. My middle name is Fern like the little girl in the book, my mother loved that book; she imagined Lance would draw that parallel, but no, instead he convinced me I was the pig. Every night, over and over, until I believed him."

"Claire, that is so fucked up."

"No shit."

"Am I the first man you've had sex with?"

"No," she replied in a whisper.

"Many?"

"No."

"Wanna tell me about it?"

"No."

"Have you slept with lots of girls?"

"Yes."

"Why?"

"Because I'm an asshole."

She laughed.

"I'm serious. I'm a selfish asshole. I knew it would never lead anywhere, but I wooed them and fucked them and broke their hearts, over and over again. Because I wanted what I wanted and I didn't care about their feelings at all."

"Why is that, do you think?"

Hurt them before they hurt you.

"Because while you were running around California thinking you were Miss Piggy, I was wandering the streets of Brooklyn thinking I was an Ourobouros," he said making a circle in the air with his finger.

She slapped her forehead with the palm of her hand. "Always feel the need to underline that you are smarter than me, huh, Peter? Ourobouros? What the fuck is Ourobouros?"

"I was a douchebag, Claire, in my twenties I read about all this kind of crap. Ourobouros is an ancient symbol, a circular serpent, it eats its own tail, it's self-sustaining. How else could I explain being alive without food?"

"Peter, I'm suddenly deeply embarrassed for you. You sound like Agent Mulder. You're not a demonic serpent thing, Peter."

"It's not demonic and you're not *of* the porcine species, Claire."

"Here we go again. Tit for tat."

They sat in silence for a while. Then Claire did some dishes, Peter read the *Herald Tribune.*

Finally Claire broke the silence. "How about we just stop talking about this stuff for a while and just live? Let's call it a draw. We're both fucked-up freaks with a million secrets," she said opening a tiny, dusty window at the back of heart just a little crack. "Who isn't by the way? And let's just enjoy Paris. How much longer are you here for?"

"How much longer are *you* here for?"

"Arrgh, Peter!!! I am going to kill you! Stop."

"As long as I want. You?"

"A little less long than that."

"Again with the mystery."

"No more questions, deal?"

He looked at her. Her skin glistened, her cheeks rosy, she suddenly looked a child negotiating a later bedtime. His eyes involuntarily shifted a notch softer.

"Deal."

Looking out the bedroom window the next morning, Claire saw a middle-aged, well-dressed woman picking leaves off the sidewalk carefully, examining each one closely, sometimes discarding ones she deemed unsuitable and placing the others into a brown leather tote.

"I'm going downstairs for a minute," she said to Peter who was absently fingering the room-temperature butter on the dining table while he read. "And stop doing that, it's disgusting," she added as she closed the front door behind her.

Claire approached the woman slowly so as not to startle her.

"Trés joli, les... um...'leaves'," Claire said pathetically.

The woman turned and stared at Claire. She was beautiful but her face was crosshatched with myriad tiny lines as if it were made of glass that had shattered and been glued back together.

"Non. Important," she replied.

"Important?" Claire queried. So far so good, the words were the same in both languages.

The woman didn't answer.

Claire reached deep for the 'why'. "Pourquoi?" she finally managed.

"Parce-que j'en ai besoin. Ce sont des cartes," came the answer.

Claire didn't get it. The woman thought they were 'cards' of some kind. She 'needed' them?

"Cards?" Claire asked in English.

"No. Maps," the woman answered flatly in English after a pause and then walked away from her.

"Maps," smiled Claire remembering now that the words for both were the same in French. She picked up a wet leaf and held it up against the sun to backlight it. The tiny veins did look like roads. She chose a few, laid them one on top of the other neatly and rolled them together tight, lengthwise like a cigarette. She put them in her pocket.

"What was that about?" Peter asked when she came back in. "You didn't even put your jacket on."

"I have something for us to smoke when we're lost. It'll help us find the way."

"No shit, Claire! You rock! You found a pot dealer in Paris.

You are the coolest."

"And you, Peter, are a stunted adolescent."

"What? No pot?"

"No, Peter, no pot."

"What then?"

"You wouldn't understand."

"Try me."

"No."

"Okay. Whatever." He turned back to the book he was reading and purposely stuck his index finger in the butter boat to annoy her.

"Infant," she sighed, running her own finger down the length of the rolled stack of leaves in her pocket.

Claire missed walking. Solitary all her life, long, exploratory walks had saved her. Despite the extra weight of her abundant flesh, she had always had surprising stamina. Lost inside her own head, she would wander for hours along dirt roads, city streets, country lanes, highways, even. Now, the limp from the accident hobbled her. Without the walks to soothe her brain, the mechanical clop-clop gone, Claire felt increasingly agitated. She needed a rhythmic gesture, something to provide a backbeat to the empty days. She decided to teach herself to crochet.

"Hi, Grandma!" Peter said sarcastically one day when he came home from yet another day browsing CDs at the FNAC (he was regressing).

"Screw you. It calms me."

He plopped down in front of her.

"Where's the other needle?"

"I'm not knitting, you idiot. It's crochet."

"Excuse-ay moi!" he teased. "Why crochet, isn't knitting

easier?"

She put it down. "No actually, it's not easier. What the hell could you possibly know about knitting?" she said, a little embarrassed.

But when she saw that Peter looked genuinely hurt, she added, "I'm sorry."

"You know, Claire, I know the accident took a lot out of you and the past few months have been pretty kooky, but give a guy a break will ya."

She exhaled, picked up the yarn and continued in a more measured tone. "I like the movement that crocheting makes, the gesture is like reaching for something. You dip into the yarn pull a piece through and build with each action. It's soothing."

"Don't get mad, but same with knitting, no?"

She thought about it. "I suppose, but with crochet, it's one needle not two. I like the singularity of it."

He looked confused.

"You know, it seems like you always need two of everything to accomplish anything; two hands, eyes, feet. There's always duality: yin and yang, night and day, good and evil, blah, blah, blah. Seems like alone, the world won't spin. I like that it's just the one little hook."

"…hook and yarn, though..." he added. "That's tw…"

Her angry look shut him up. He backed down and changed course.

"Whatcha makin'?" he asked innocuously.

"A road," she answered picking up the yarn again.

She had chosen a deep, red wool. Crimson. She loved red. Always had. As she crocheted, her thoughts involuntarily drifted back to Lance. One year, on his birthday, mere minutes after he had gleefully opened it, she had stolen all the various reds out of her brother's giant *Crayola* crayon box: *Red, Red Orange, Scarlett, Radical Red, Jazzberry Jam, Hot Magenta, Brick Red, Cerise* and her favorite: *Razzmatazz.*

She had often hid his precious things, mouse to his lion, she knew of no other way to hurt him. He knew it was her doing and was furious. He had searched everywhere to no avail. It was summer, hot and dry. She had planted the crayons in the back yard along the side of the house, pushed them down into the crackling earth so that only the top flat circles of color could be seen, like strewn petals. When he was out at baseball practice she would uproot them and draw all manner of pulsating hearts on long sheets of paper towel. She would then roll them back up and place them back in the kitchen. Thinking it was just a pattern in the print, neither her mother nor Lance ever noticed that they were cleaning up life's little messes with a million permutations of her heart.

Now, Claire could not stop crocheting. Her project was about a foot wide and immeasurably long. As she progressed she would roll the other end back up, much like the paper towels of her childhood. Peter helped her move one of the big armchairs from the living room to the bedroom so she could keep the ever-growing roll in a corner, tethered to her like a giant round buoy, but wooly.

She knew Peter was unnerved by all this, but ignored the searching stare that burned like a hot lamp over her bent head. He'd often just leave the apartment without a word. She left him to his own devices so that he would leave her to hers. She knew he spent most days lurking in the sex shops of Pigalle. Claire had stopped having sex with Peter a few weeks ago. Her emotions had gotten too complicated for her to manage. The last time she had been overwhelmed by emotion, the results had been disastrous. She was terrified of herself. One night as he went to slip his buttered fingers into her vagina, she had simply grabbed his hand and said, "No." For now, she was happy that he had found another outlet and she took comfort in the soft yarn. She poured her tumbled feelings into it, the tight pattern began to take the shape of her DNA, or at least, that's what she imagined.

"Let's go out and get shitfaced," Peter said one evening out of the blue. He had been sitting there for over an hour numbly staring at her while she crocheted.

"What?" she asked, not looking up.

"You heard me, let's get lit, wasted, bombed, soused, three-sheets-to-the-wind, you know, drunk as skunks."

"Why would we do that?"

"Because we haven't gotten drunk together since the night of the accident. I think it would do us some good."

"Good in what way?"

"If you need to ask me that, then you *definitely* need a drink. Where do you wanna go? C'mon, it'll be fun."

Claire was at a loss. Because of Peter's eating (or more precisely, *not* eating) they never went out to restaurants. They 'ate' dinner at home. Claire would make herself something and Peter would sit with her at the table and have a beer or a coffee or nothing. But he did sit with her, and she appreciated that. Though she never did say so.

"I really don't feel like it."

"Claire, listen. Things are getting depressing. You just sit around and knit all d..."

"Crochet."

"...crochet all day and I, well um...I'm out. And we don't have sex anymore and we don't even really talk. It sucks."

"Peter, are you breaking up with me?" Claire said sarcastically, again masking fear.

"Hardy, fucking har, Claire."

"We're not a couple, Peter. I told you from the start. If you want to leave; leave."

Peter clenched his jaw in aggravation and did a theatrical exhale to calm himself, and then continued, articulating exaggeratedly, as if he were talking to a petulant five-year-old. "Claire. I will remind you, that this is my apartment, well, at least that I am paying for this apartment, *in which you live.* I also do pay for groceries and EVERY OTHER DAMN THING. How exactly do you expect to survive without me?!"

"I have family here," she replied matter-of-factly.

Pause.

"Where?"

"In Paris."

"Are you shitting me?"

"I shit you not," she said perfunctorily, not looking up. Her heart banged against her chest like a pounding fist. She let a thin sliver of air escape from her nose to calm herself. She immediately regretted having said anything at all, but he had been a bully and she simply hadn't been able to stop herself from fighting back.

She knew Peter's mouth was hanging involuntarily open. She had heard its wet pop, but she ignored it.

"Oh, Peter, stop being so dramatic."

"Why didn't you tell me?"

"You didn't ask."

"Oh, my *GOD*!! We had a non-asking deal thingy! How can you hold that against me?"

"I'm not holding it against you. I'm explaining why you didn't know."

Silence.

"It's why I came to Paris," she continued. "Why did *you* come to Paris by the way?" she added casually, attempting as she often did, to catch him off-guard and unearth a truth.

"No big mystery! To try and friggin' eat, Claire!"

"Oh, and how's that going for you?" She felt like hurting him.

He clenched his hands on his knees.

"Claire. This makes NO sense. At the hospital they said they couldn't contact relatives..." he paused, his mind racing. "Why did I pay the hospital bill? Why are you living in my fucking house?!"

"It's not your house."

"Claire!!"

"Oh, Peter, relax. It's complicated."

"Isn't everything with regards to you?"

She leveled a stare at him.

"Claire, I am not kidding, if you deflect this conversation by alluding to my not eating so help me, I will fucking knock your teeth out."

"Oh not my teeth. I love my teeth," she said calmly, her old defenses, back again.

He stood up and hovered over her. For the first time since they had met she had the fleeting sensation that if pushed, he just might hit her.

"Okay, maybe you're right. Let's drink," she offered.

"Yeah, whatever. I'll be at the bar on rue des Bernardins, but don't come down unless you're ready to spill everything. I'm really fucking tired of these continual dramatic reveals. This is real life, Claire."

"Is it now?" she asked calmly and then, looking up, "Hungry?"

In one swift motion he got up, grabbed his keys, walked out the front door and slammed it hard. Three seconds, tops. A small cactus he had bought her toppled off the table next to her as if fainting from the violence of his exit.

She exhaled forcefully in its direction; the tiny cactus somehow tipped back to an upright position. She was shaken but oddly content. She'd often seen couples fight in restaurants, bars, on the street; she craved the petty horror of it all; even in those bleak moments, she had envied that intimacy.

So this is how women do it, she thought to herself.

She decided to take her time going down to meet him. She showered, and lingered putting her make-up on. She had gotten really good at it. While Peter went in search of sex, she'd sometimes put down her yarn and secretly head out to the big department stores on the *Grand Boulevards*. She loved them; they looked like ancient palaces, or giant ornate dollhouses. Inside she would play with the make-up like a kid with finger paints, sometimes she let the pretty salesgirls show her how; they kept suggesting taupes and browns to compliment her russet complexion.

"Trés chic!" they'd exclaim proudly showing her the result in the mirror, but no sale; she always wanted crimson lips, deep red. And for her eyelids she always chose green…khaki, celadon, emerald, whatever, but always green, to match her eyes. In her mind she thought to herself, *That way, even when they are closed, they are open.*

She pulled on a new black dress. It was soft cotton and loose, but the empire waist cut revealed her breasts in a suggestive manner, pushing them up Marie-Antoinette style; she looked down at them, they looked like moons.

He was sitting in a corner table by the window, his chin resting on his left hand while his right fingered the edge of the short glass in front of him. He really was very handsome. She remembered the tightening in her stomach when she had first seen him on the plane.

"My oh my, why did I pick today to become a man?" she had wondered, before reminding herself that either way she would have been invisible to him.

She took her coat off wordlessly and stood in front of him. She wanted to be admired.

"Did I pay for that?" he barked, pointing at the dress.

She sat down, deflated.

"This isn't a fucking date, Claire. What the fuck?" He was

already drunk.

Claire rightly assumed he'd done a few fast shots to steady his nerves.

"Are you playing me? Are you after my money? What are you? A con-artist?" he asked quickly and agitatedly. "You know I thought about that the very first time I let you…Dallas…into my flat. I thought, *What the hell am I doing? This guy is a total stranger, he could be a killer, he could be a thief…*"

"He could be a woman," she suggested helpfully.

Peter hung his head. "No, Claire, *that,* I hadn't thought of." And then, "Ok. I've had it with this shit. Get yourself a drink, fuckwad and then spill it. All."

"*Fuckwad*? Peter, please don't talk to me like that. Really." She felt a mix of fear and deep, extreme panic.

"Don't act all shocked, you lying manipulative cunt. I don't know what the fuck you're up to but it stops tonight."

Claire's eyes filled with tears.

"Don't you fucking *dare* pull that pussy shit on me. Talk!"

Claire closed her eyes once, and two perfect, egg-shaped tears rolled out of each of her green eyes, like tiny tsunamis of grief.

"You're going to be disappointed, Lance. It's all really very mundane." She didn't notice the slip. Neither did he.

"I'm waiting," he said over-loudly in an effort to compensate for the slight softening he had felt when she had closed her eyes for that brief heartbreaking instant.

"After my brother's death, I did a lot of walking." She paused. "Can I get a glass of water?"

"Stop stalling," he said, but pointed to a carafe on the bar and made a pouring gesture to the waiter.

"I would walk and walk. It calmed me I guess. Often I had no idea where I was going, I'd just walk."

"I get the picture, Forrest Gump, keep going," he said sarcastically, determined not to be swayed.

"One day when I was thirteen, on one of my walks, a man

pulled me into a doorway and raped me."

"What do you mean?" he said, furrowing his brow.

"What do you mean, what do I mean? Could that sentence be any clearer?" she asked flatly.

They stared at each other in silence.

Finally, she took a sip of water and reflexively glanced around the bar in that way one does to be sure the coast is clear; but then, instead of leaning forward in a conspiratorial gesture, she leaned protectively back, her arms folded across her chest, and began:

"A man pulled me into a doorway and raped me. In broad daylight, on a street I'd walked down a million times, in a nice neighborhood, in my hometown. It was a red metal door between the dry cleaners and the 7-11. It felt like a video game, or *Chutes and Ladders*; a door opened as I walked by, an arm reached out yanked me into a narrow hallway." She was recounting without emotion, in an even rhythmic tone, squinting slightly, as if she were reading letters off an eye chart. "I was wearing an oversized t-shirt for a dress, I was so fat that was pretty much all I could wear in the summer back then. It happened really fast. He yanked down my underwear, pushed me against the wall, stuck it in, pumped a few times, pulled it out, and shoved me back out into the street, slamming the door behind me."

"What did you do?" Peter managed.

"Nothing. I kept walking." She paused. " His cum started to trickle down my leg. I didn't know what to do. So I kept walking. No one noticed. No one ever looked at me anyway."

"Did you tell your parents?"

"No. I didn't tell anyone."

"Claire, why?"

"Because I had killed my brother, Peter. I thought it was karmic payback."

"I'm so sorry," he said wanting to touch her arm, but didn't.

"What does this all have to do with Paris?"

She took a sip of water.

"Peter. I got pregnant."

"My God."

"I know." She almost laughed. "I couldn't believe it. I mean what are the odds?"

"No shit," he said pushing his chair and leaning back.

"It gets worse, Peter."

"Are you trying to freak me out?"

"No, but you wanted it all, so have it all."

"Fair enough."

She leaned forward and took a sip of whiskey, leaving the red print of her lips on the edge of the glass.

"I was a kid. I was very fat. I had no idea what was going on, like all those stupid people you read about in the tabloids; like that girl who shat her baby out at the Prom."

In a weak attempt to lighten the moment, Peter smiled.

She mistakenly thought he was making fun of her, so she shaped her next sentence into a fist. "I had the baby in my parents' bathroom, two feet away from where I dumped my brother's body."

Peter couldn't stop himself recoiling slightly from the table.

"I was terrified. In my twisted, panicked brain, as it was happening, I thought Lance was coming back through me. But it was a girl. Thankfully. When my father came home and saw me on the ground in the bathroom covered in blood with a baby in my arms, he went completely nuts." She paused and looked at the wall behind Peter's head. She knew eye contact wouldn't be possible. "I mean, seriously insane." And then, very quickly, in one breath: "He grabbed a bottle of my mother's perfume, jammed it up me and kicked me in the crotch over and over. '*You stink of...rotten, rotten!*' he yelled again and again, covering his nose as he kicked. Inside me, I could feel the glass shattering." She kept her eyes on the wall.

"My God, Claire, this can't be the truth."

"It is." She drank some more water, still looking past him, as if blind. "They thought I was a little slut. They didn't even ask who the father might be. My mother took her away and left her in an unzipped dufflebag at the local train station, to be found. My father never spoke to me again. Ever. Not a single word. It was as if I was invisible."

"Jesus."

"Yep." She touched her lips absently, and they stained the tips of her fingers red. "I came to Paris because I had a lead on someone I thought was my daughter."

"Wow. Was she?"

Claire looked at her fingertips questioningly. "No."

"I'm sorry."

"It's not your fault. I have always wondered why people do that all the time."

"What?"

"Apologize for things that aren't their fault. And conversely not take responsibility for those that are."

"Is that a dig at me?"

"No, Peter. You've been pretty amazing to be honest. I don't think anyone has ever been so nice to me. Except when I was Dallas for that brief period, people liked me then, liked me better as a man," she said in an almost sing-song-y tone. Her walls were up again.

"So you don't have family here? The whole *I can manage on my own* speech was a bullshit bluff?" Peter asked forcing his mind back to the beginning.

"I can manage on my own. Always have."

Peter felt drained, more exhausted than he could remember being for a long time, almost drugged. His eyelids felt heavy; he looked down at his glass. It was empty.

"I'm wiped out. Let's go home."

"Home?"

"Yes, Claire. Home." He got up and helped her with her coat.

He stood very close behind her.

"You smell good, Claire. You always smell good."

She turned to look at him.

"Thank you for that, Peter."

"I mean it."

"I know."

Back in the apartment they got ready for bed without a word. Peter had unconsciously kept his hands in loose fists on the table for most of her story, both left and right, a short distance apart. He was likely just steadying himself, or keeping them at the ready to tighten into a punch if need be, but to her he looked like someone in a cartoon waiting eagerly for a plate of food to be placed in front of them, fork and knife sticking straight up out of either clenched hand. But there was no cutlery in Peter's life, just small oval holes formed by thumb and forefinger, like eyes (or eggs), where the utensils should have been. She suddenly felt sorry for him.

"Go to the bedroom," she said.

"You can't possibly be serious."

"No, not that. I mean *take* the bedroom. I'll sleep on the couch tonight. It's only fair."

"Fair? You spend three months fucking with my head worse than skunk weed and you give me the bed as compensation? Generous."

"Please," she said, sensing that he wasn't being mean, just scared. "I don't know what else do to for you tonight."

She made a sweeping gesture towards the bedroom with her hand. "Please."

"Fine. Whatever. I'm exhausted." And then more softly, "Goodnight, Claire."

"Goodnight, Peter."

"The sheets smell like you," he shouted a few minutes later through the closed door. "In a good way," he added after a beat.

She sat on the couch and waited a few minutes more, then she went into the small kitchen, tore a big black trash bag from the roll they kept under the sink and slowly, quietly and methodically threw out every morsel of food.

She cleaned out the cupboards, the fridge, tossed the condiments, salt and pepper too; everything but some ground coffee, milk and a half-empty carton of orange juice. She stood in the kitchen doorway the bag bulging, and looked around the living room, she remembered a *Bounty* bar (she liked coconut) in her purse; she rummaged for it and threw it away too. She opened the front door carefully and dragged the bag as quietly as she could down the stairs to the basement garbage.

Upstairs, she unfolded the convertible sofa and lay down. It was pretty comfortable but there was a small gap between the top edge of the mattress and the back of the couch. She had forgotten to get the pillows Peter always used out of the bedroom closet and as a result her head tilted backwards at an awkward angle.

"Shit," she said to herself and turned on her side.

She smiled in the dark.

"Goodbye, shit."

She wanted Peter. She needed Peter. She had read in *Glamour* magazine that couples often attributed happy marriages to the sharing of common interests.

Claire had decided to stop eating.

Not used to the bed and bothered by the shadows that floated across the ceiling in the curtain-less living room like storm clouds, Claire slept restlessly, alternating between vibrant dreams and insomnia. At 6:15 a.m. she gave up, got up and made a pot of coffee and picked up her crochet. Around 9 a.m. Peter emerged.

"Hi," he said, still half asleep.

"Hi, I made coffee, want some?" she said, brightly.

"Sure."

She poured him a cup and they sat at the table and drank in silence. They often did this; shared liquids together. They looked like an ordinary couple. Almost.

"You must be hungry, with…well with…(she searched) everything, you didn't have dinner last night did you?"

"I'm not hungry, Claire," he said fixing her with a flat stare.

She looked away, quietly mourning the loss of normalcy in the moment.

"Why don't we go for a walk? It's sunny," he offered.

Claire glanced at the gigantic roll of crocheted yarn in the corner.

"Claire, if I felt I could handle another emotional atomic bomb this morning, I'd ask you to explain what the fuck that's all about, but I'm frankly not up for it. C'mon, let's go get some air. It'll do us both good."

Claire was hesitant.

"We'll walk slowly," he said.

"Ok," Claire answered, moved that he had grasped the reason for her reticence.

"You wanna take the first shower, or should I?" he asked.

"I'll take it. I didn't get much sleep, I need to wash off the dream dust."

"The *dream dust*? What are you, nine?"

"God, Peter, didn't your parents instill any whimsy in you at all?"

"No," he replied immediately. "Did yours? Your childhood didn't sound like too much of a fairy tale last night."

"No it wasn't." She forced her defenses down. She took a minute to watch them back away like an army, retreating. "But when I was really, really little, once in a while, when I had trouble getting out of bed in the morning, my mom would say, *'C'mon kiddo, shake off that dream dust and dig into the day.'* And I'd get up and shake my hair around like a dog shaking off water, and we'd both laugh."

"So this was before she took your newborn child and left it in a gym bag by the train tracks?"

Claire stared at him silently and then got up and walked toward the bathroom.

"I'm sorry. I'M SORRY, okay?!" he bellowed at her back as she walked away.

She took a long, very hot shower. It calmed her. She loved combing her wet hair. It was almost to her shoulders now. She liked the feeling of the tips; dripping, they licked her collarbone like little tongues.

She got dressed and headed back into the living room. Peter was sitting on the edge of the couch with a look of frank panic on his face.

"What the hell are you doing, Claire?"

"What?"

"Where's the food?" he asked as calmly as he could manage.

"Why were you looking for food?"

"That's not the point. Where is it?"

"It's gone. I'm done with it."

"Claire."

"Peter, do you secretly eat while I shower?" she asked, but she already knew the answer. A month or so ago, every day, she'd counted every cookie, every carrot, every everything edible she had brought into the house, to test him. He had passed.

In high school, too distracted to study for tests, she'd often scribbled crib notes on the tops of her wide thighs, pulling the long t-shirt up, just enough to read the words etched there in blue ink. She imagined Peter had an inventive way of cheating too. He had to. How else?

"Claire, stop trying to turn the conversation around, you always do that, it's infuriating. What are you DOING?" he yelled.

"I'm done with food."

Peter hung his head. "You are the most exhausting human being I have ever met. You can't just stop eating, Claire. You know that."

"No I don't know that. You did it."

"Yes, but it's different for me."

Claire felt a wave of heat rise up her back, was this the moment? Would he finally explain it all? Would he love her enough to trust her?

"Why?" she managed.

"Believe me, I wish I knew," he answered offhandedly. "Claire," he said purposefully. "Please don't. It's just dumb. What's the point?"

The hope inside her evaporated, sizzled away instantly like a drop of water flicked on a hot pan.

"I like the idea of being self-sustained," she answered.

"You are truly nuts. No, I mean really, right? Like unstable."

She opened her mouth to respond; but he had already had more than he could take.

"Whatever, Claire, it's your life. I guess."

"What do you mean *'I guess'*? It is my life."

"Yes, it is. And mine is mine and I'm not sure how much more of your bullshit I am willing to swallow. Let's go walk."

"Fine."

She got her jacket, he put on his coat and they went downstairs. He held the door to the street open for her.

As she walked through he said, "Claire."

"Yes."

"Just walking, no talking."

She nodded.

They set off. A few paces on, she slipped her arm through his to steady herself.

He let her.

The first forty-eight hours, she was euphoric. She felt no hunger at all. She felt clean and light and she loved it. Happiness was just around the corner, she saw it once, in her mind's eye, early one morning…happiness…it was small, round like a hopping bunny and smelled like fresh cream. But soon, much to her dismay, she started to feel the effects of food deprivation, some dizziness, lack of focus, tired mostly and also, oddly nausea. She pushed them away by drinking juice and water, after all Peter did too. Somehow, perhaps through sheer determination, she lasted nearly two weeks. She lost about 11 lbs.

Peter seeing the weight loss, her pale face. He would shake his head.

"My life," she would say to his turned back.

"Not for long," he'd answer.

Crocheting, she'd often look at her wrists. They were lovely, delicate now. As the fat melted away and her skeleton emerged, she felt that for the first time she was truly discovering herself. Seeing the structure, the foundation of her being, was reassuring. She imagined architects must feel this way on building sites, seeing the beams of their imagined buildings take shape, comforted knowing that they were being erected on solid foundations.

Her loose dresses hid the extent of the weight loss from Peter. Had he known how close to the precipice she was, he would have intervened. Unworried by death, stepping out of the shower, she secretly relished in seeing her body morph, her skeleton emerge, as her flesh shifted on her frame. Her legs thinned as did her arms and neck, but her breasts became even more prominent, she was so delighted by them that she didn't wonder why.

Then one day, admiring herself naked in the mirror, she suddenly saw. It was like seeing a gray hair for the first time; likely there a while, but somehow previously unnoticed.

She stood there, immobile, fixed in place as if someone behind her had unexpectedly yelled, *'Freeze'!*

"My God," she said out loud, horrified. Then, softly, in beatific wonder, "*My* God."

She dressed and went to wait for Peter on the couch. When she heard his key in the door, she reflexively pulled her knees up to her chest protectively.

"Hey there," he said pulling off his scarf, not looking at her.

Silence. He turned.

"Wow. You look like you saw a ghost. You okay?"

"I'm scared."

"Told you so," he said, gloating; he lit a cigarette. "I hear you should start with soup first, don't jump right to a cheeseburger, it'll make you barf."

"No, it's not that."

"Come on, Claire, you look like shit."

"I think I'm pregnant, Peter."

The cigarette involuntarily slipped out of his fingers and rolled to the ground. He jumped up and searched for it under the armchair. He beat the rug with his hand to ensure the scattered embers were all out.

He sat back down and looked at her. He was speechless. Finally, she simply stood up in front of him and pulled her long, loose black dress up to her breasts and revealed a still small, yet unmistakable, basketball-shaped bump.

He reached out in wonder to touch it with his right hand.

"I don't know…what…to say," he stammered. "I'm not sure how I feel. My gut reaction is sheer panic. Fuck, am I one of those cowardly assholes? Of course, I am. I have always been an asshole, right?" He got up and paced the room, rapidly unraveling. "I mean, but we're not a couple, I don't have to be happy, this isn't one of those fucking *Hallmark* moments. My God, how much weirder could this shit get? A baby?! But, we haven't had sex in months! What are you…like, four months along? What are we going t…"

"Peter." She interrupted his hysterical rant.

"I know. I'm freaking out," he said anxiously.

"Peter. I'm really scared."

"Me too, but people do this all the time, right?"

"Peter, I have no ovaries."

"Jesus. H. Christ." He dropped to the ground into a seated cross-legged position like a kid around a campfire and leaned forward onto his legs for comfort.

From her standing position, Claire spoke to the top of his head. "The thing with my father…the bottle, the broken glass. The doctors had to take everything out. I haven't had a period in twenty years. I've got nothing in there. At all. I can't be pregnant, Peter, it's impossible."

He laughed nervously. "I give up," he said. "You win."

"Win what?"

"Whatever game this is you're playing."

"It's not a game. I'm scared."

Peter got up and walked to the window.

"Do you feel pregnant?"

She put her hands on her stomach. "I don't know. I don't know what being pregnant feels like."

"Well, I know what being pregnant looks like, and you are definitely pregnant." He tapped the window repeatedly with his index finger, as if nudging it to provide some sort of answer. "Fucking hell, Claire! Are you sure?"

"Yes, Peter. I went to see a doctor, doctors. Many. I talked infertility options; they all looked me incredulously across their big desks as if I were insane. '*Miss Anderson, there is categorically no way at all for you to get pregnant, you don't have the female parts necessary for baby-making,*' one of them told me in an effort to dumb it down into language that I could understand. I desperately wanted a child, maybe to replace the one that had been taken, maybe to resurrect my brother in some fucked-up way. I tried everything. There is no way. I don't understand what's happening." She looked over at the giant roll of yarn, it looked like a nest; she fought the urge to burrow into it.

"I need to think." He went into the bedroom and closed the door. After half an hour he came back.

"You need to leave," he said plainly.

"Peter."

"Claire. You need to leave. I don't know you. I met you on a plane. This is the last straw. It's too much. I feel like you are making me insane. I want you gone." His voice was hard, but he searched for his cigarettes, and avoided her eyes.

Claire felt oddly calm. "You of all people, Peter. The unexplainable?"

"Tonight. Take your stuff and leave. You told me you could manage on your own. Do."

She felt her spine stiffen, she bowed her head slightly, she looked at the crochet hook that had made its way into her hand somehow and noted the similarity between her and it; both made of metal, both with their 'heads' hung forward in shame. Or pain.

"Okay, fine," she said, quietly.

Wordlessly, she got up and started gathering her things. A few black dresses, her beloved make-up, her teeth whiteners. She filled her black backpack and put the rest in garbage bags, she had no other luggage. She stood in the doorway. Peter was staring out the window with his back to her.

"Okay, 'bye," she said.

He turned and pointed to the gigantic roll of woven yarn in the corner.

"What about that?" he asked.

"Throw it out. I don't need it anymore," she answered.

They stared at each other. He broke the stare and looked around the room.

"Do you want the cactus?"

"No, it's just like you. Keep it." She thought he might respond, but he didn't. "I'm gonna go now," she finally said.

"Good."

She opened the door and walked through.

"Claire."

"Yes?"

"Eat something."

She closed the door behind her and walked down the steps with the pack on her back and a garbage bag in each hand. She walked, limping more than usual under the weight, towards a nearby hotel she had stayed in as Dallas during her first days in Paris. It was small and cheap and charmless, the sort of place young and lost people crashed into.

"Une chambre s'il vous plait," she said to the man at the front desk. His hands were dirty. She recognized him. He did not recognize her.

Once in the room, an impossibly dingy, cell-like space on the top floor, she took off her coat and folded it over the solitary chair. She heard the ping of something metal hitting the wood floor. It was her key to Peter's apartment. She had forgotten to give it back. He had forgotten to ask for it.

She called down to the front desk and asked for the room-service menu. The hotel had no room service.

"I'm pregnant. I need something to eat, I don't feel well," She told the man flatly, in English.

He took pity and brought her up some bread and water.

She ate the baguette slowly and purposefully, chewing each bite into a sort of dough dust before swallowing.

She lay down on the bed on her back and pulled up her dress

and looked down at her stomach. It was very taut. Thin blue veins, zigged this way and that across it; like roads on a map. Her eyes drifted to the ceiling, there was a wet patch in the corner; something brown was seeping from above. Maybe the roof had a leak.

She was cold. She got up and put her jacket on. She pulled it tight across her stomach. She felt a warmth spread within her.

"Baby," she whispered. "Come, little man, come."

She rooted around her bag and found the pen she and Peter had often used to do the crossword puzzles. Because she had no paper, she wrote to her unborn child on the glossy pages of the crumpled fashion magazine that she found scrunched in the bottom of her purse. She sat on the edge of the bed, placed the bound cluster of shiny paper awkwardly on her knees and wrote across a shampoo ad.

Dear Little,

Once, riding in a taxi, years ago, I looked out of the window. Rolling slowly past…the people in the street looked like dancers, dancing, graceful, each one. Mundane gestures, steps; suddenly rhythmic, fluid. I could see their teeth so clearly, so white, everyone was smiling. Off in the far distance I could hear an orchestra playing; violins mostly, and an oboe.

I want to dance, Little.

Come be my partner.

Don't worry, you will know me; I'll be the one with the lips the color of your heart.

See you soon.

I love you.

Your mother,

Claire Fern Anderson

Peter remained immobile in the apartment after Claire's departure for hours. He had wanted her gone and she was. But still, it had all happened faster than he'd expected. He was shaken. He sat, loosely gripping the couch, as if anticipating and aftershock. "Goddamn it, I can still fucking smell you," he said and got up to open a window.

He looked out onto the quiet street. He turned and looked back at the empty apartment. He had no idea what to do next.

He poured himself a whiskey and called his mother.

"Mom?"

"Peter?"

"Yes."

"Peter?"

"Yes."

"My son Peter?

"Yes, Mom. What the hell?"

"It's just I'd forgotten what you sound like, it's been so long."

"Don't start."

"Your father keeps putting money in your account. I would have stopped two months ago. What do you want?"

"Mom, life is weird, huh?"

"Peter, are you stoned again?"

"No, Mom, I am not stoned."

"Are you coming home?"

"I don't know."

"Have you written a book?"

"What?"

"Have you written a book? That's why you went to Paris, remember? To write. Have you written?"

"No," he said sheepishly.

"Didn't think so."

"Thanks for the vote of confidence."

"Well, I was right wasn't I?"

"Mom, can I ask you a question?"

"No, I have not had any Botox."

He laughed.

"Sorry, just a reflex." He thought he heard a smile in her voice.

"Mom, was I normal kid?"

"What do you mean by normal?"

"You know – normal. Did I have any weird psychological shit going on, or health issues?"

"Well, you were always kind of an asshole."

"Mom!"

"I mean it, even at three you were an asshole. You always thought you were special."

"In what way?"

"I don't know, superior. Like the rules didn't apply to you."

"What rules?"

"You know the rules. Life. I think we were too lenient."

"That's it?"

"Yes, I suppose that's it. Just an asshole."

They were both quiet for a while.

"Peter…"

"Yes, I know…manicure? Massage?"

"Facial."

"Okay, don't be late."

Silence again.

"Mom?"

"Yes, Peter."

"I love you."

"Oh boy, you're really in trouble this time."

"What makes you say that?"

"I just know."

"How?"

"Because I made you."

She hung up. He held the phone in his hand and looked at it as if he had never seen a phone before. Then he threw it across the room, hard. It bounced off the yarn roll and smacked him on the side of face.

"Fuck you. FUCK. YOU!" he yelled at the blood-red fuzzy blob.

The yarn loomed like a giant misshapen anatomical heart in the corner. He walked over to it; he tugged at it and stretched out a piece of it with both his hands. When pulled wide, the crocheted weave looked like a net.

"Is this a trap?" he asked it, questioningly.

He pawed at it.

He went over to the kitchen to make himself a drink. As he grabbed a glass, he noticed that his hands were very red. He flipped both palms up, they were stained a deep dark scarlet.

The glass shattered across the counter. "Cheap fucking yarn," he reasoned.

He drank half a bottle of Jack Daniels and went to bed. He slept fitfully, dreaming an expected wild, jumbled amalgam of images. He woke up the next morning, tense. He lay in bed trying to discern the odd feeling in his stomach. He was frightened. He glanced nervously around the room, searching; he didn't know for what. He forced himself to get up. His foot tangled in something on the floor, he reached down to pick it up. It was one of Claire's long, black cotton dresses. Suddenly everything flooded back in a cold, messy rush, like a thick wave coming in faster than expected, it buckled his knees. He sat back down on the edge of the bed. He put the dress up to his face and inhaled. Her. He lay back on the bed and draped the dress over himself, as if her ghost were lying on top of him. He wrapped his arms around himself.

"What have I done?" he whispered.

After a while, he went to bathroom to splash some water on his face. He steadied himself on the sink. He looked at himself in the mirror. He needed a shave. His left eye itched, so he rubbed it. He blinked a few times; it still itched. He leaned forward and pulled down the bottom lid, he looked closely, deep into his own eyes, and after retrieving the offending lash, noticed something. Yellow. A ring of gold around each pupil; he wondered how it was possible that he had never noticed before.

He stepped out of his clothes and into the shower. He let the warm water soothe him for a few minutes then switched it to cold, very cold. It sharpened his senses, his body tensed against the onslaught, goose bumps rose on his skin and he felt his breath coming faster, but he endured. Cold. Cold. His jaw started to hammer involuntarily; he heard his teeth snap against each other. Colder. Finally, he turned off the water and stepped out. He stood naked in front of the mirror, hunched forward slightly, his stomach muscles tensed. He took forced breaths through clenched teeth, his lips pulled back in a kind of snarl.

"What beast are you, Peter Howland?" he asked of himself. "What beast?!"

He grabbed a towel and rubbed himself almost raw in an effort to heat up again.

He dressed and went into the living room. As he passed the small dining table, he was compelled to look down. Written on its glass top in crimson lipstick he saw four words:

I DO LOVE YOU.

Peter looked for her everywhere. He retraced their every step, went to every café, every bar, every shop; twice, three times. More. He didn't find her.

One night, about three weeks after she'd gone…after he'd told her to go, he found himself obscenely drunk in the bar downstairs. He was slumped in a corner, his forehead against the window, his labored breath frosting the glass, he absently drew the letter 'C' onto the cold window with the tip of his finger and noticed, even in his haze that it looked like a semi-circle, half an egg.

He missed her.

"Allez, you go now," said the barman.

Peter ignored him. The lights switched off in the back part of the bar. It was closing time.

"Allez, allez, you go."

"Go where?" Peter asked.

"Go home. I know you live right near, non?"

Peter closed his eyes. The barman slammed his hand flat on the table loudly.

"Hey, hey calmez-vous, Antoine." An old woman shuffled over and sat in front of Peter.

"Honey, you're English right?"

"American," he answered, his eyes half closed.

"Me too!" she said cheerfully. "From Tennessee. Originally, that is. Been here for over fifty years. Guess I'm a Frenchie now."

Peter slumped forward and put his head on the table like a kid taking a nap on his desk at school.

"C'mon, son, go back where you belong, it's sleepy time," she said in her southern drawl.

Peter sat bolt upright and looked right at her. It startled her. He grabbed his jacket, stood up, patted her on the top of the head as if she were a good dog and sped out of the bar.

Even though he knew it would be open late, he ran all the way there. For some unknown reason, he'd checked the 'Claire' places, but not the 'Dallas' places. Dallas existed in his head, but not his heart, and it was his heart that had been guiding him.

He got to the door, threw 20€ at the bouncer and ran down the stairs. He frantically scanned the room for Claire. Nothing. He walked around looking in every recessed corner; he checked the ladies' room *and* the men's room. In desperation, he even looked *under* the big red couch in the back room, but no Claire.

He felt completely deflated; inside his chest, he thought he felt a rubbery flutter, like a torn balloon. He dropped into a deep, foul-smelling armchair by the bar.

"Doooode. No way," he heard a voice say.

He looked up. It was Glory.

He shook his head and laughed at the irony.

"What. Is. Up. Dude?" she said punctuating each word excitedly. He sensed it was a rhetorical question. He didn't answer.

"Haven't seen you in a while, still in Paris, huh? What was your name again?"

"Peter."

"Mine's Glo…"

"I know. I remember the story. How's tricks Glory?"

"What do you mean?"

"I mean how are tricks? How's business? Has whoring been affected by the recession?" He was in a nasty mood.

She took a reflexive step away from him.

"That's weird, dude. I remembered you as being one of the good guys. You okay?"

"No, Glory. I am not okay. I am not even remotely okay."

"Wanna talk about it?"

"Most definitely not."

"Are you sure? I find it helps to get stuff off your chest sometimes."

He looked up at her. Her hair was a little longer than last time. Her breasts were still as amazing; she was wearing a tight t-shirt. He squinted in the dark to read the lettering: DALLAS COWBOYS.

"Un-fucking believable," he said, laughing despite himself.

"What? What's funny?" she smiled.

"Nothing," he said, shaking his head incredulously. "Want a drink?"

She hesitated.

"C'mon. I *am* one of the good guys. Don't be afraid."

"Okay," she conceded.

He handed her some money. "Get me a Jack. Neat. And get

yourself whatever you want."

"Jack and Coke?"

"Whatever you want."

She skipped over to the bar. When she brought back the drinks, he noticed that she had pocketed the change. They drank in silence.

"So, what have you been up to? You like it here, huh? Paris."

"No small talk, Glory. I'm not in the mood."

"Grumpasaurus Rex," she said, pouting.

"How old are you?"

"Twenty-one."

"Of course."

It must have been a slow night for her because she sat with him for a few more rounds. Finally, drunk on top of his earlier drunk, he got up to leave. He wobbled and knocked over the low table between them.

"Whoa, dude. You are lit."

"I'm fine."

He made his way to the stairs, up them, and out onto the street. She followed him. On the sidewalk, he hesitated, not sure which way to head.

"Do you live far?" she asked.

"I live in Brooklyn."

"That's not walking distance," she answered, deadpan. "I live around the corner, wanna come to my place?" She twirled a lock of her hair suggestfully between two fingers.

Peter tried to focus his drunken vision a little; he squinted at her. She had a jacket and a scarf on, together they obstructed some of the letters on her t-shirt so that it read: ALL COW.

Peter started laughing uncontrollably, so hard that he had to sit down on the curb.

"What?" she asked defensively. "Guys think I'm pretty hot, you know."

"I'm sorry. It's just that..." He pointed at her chest and started laughing again. She looked down at herself, confused, searching for the joke.

"I don't get it," she said. "Whatever." She started walking away from him.

"Wait," he called after her. "I'm coming."

"I'm not sure anymore."

"How much?"

She didn't answer.

"How much do you charge?"

"You are most definitely not one of the good guys."

"So I have been told. I'm an asshole," he said waving his arms wide as if introducing himself to an audience, "but I won't hurt you," he added.

She didn't look convinced.

"I promise," he said sobering up for a second and looking her deep in the eyes.

She started walking away, but made a 'follow me' gesture with her hand behind her back.

Peter trundled behind her like a lost stray.

As soon as she opened the front door, she went straight into the bathroom to pee. Led by only the dim light escaping from under the closed bathroom door, Peter stumbled towards what he assumed was a couch and fell asleep instantly, curled up tight, like a fetus.

He woke to her mouth on his penis. He had a terrible hangover, too exhausted to protest, he let her. Just before he was about to come, she expertly rolled a condom on him with her mouth and sat on him in what felt like a single gesture. A rush of memory flooded over him. He closed his eyes tight, two tears rolled out of each corner as he came.

"You look like crap," she said immediately afterwards.

"Why, thank you."

"No, seriously, you look corpse-y."

"Corpse-y?" he rolled his eyes theatrically backward into his head.

She giggled. "You're weird." And then added, "I'm hungry. Aren't you?"

Peter put his hands over his ears.

"Really, really weird," she said, standing up.

She went out to get them some fresh bread for breakfast. He left her more money than she had asked for, and on the mirror by the front door with a glittery golden lip-gloss he had found in her bathroom he drew a circle. He had started a 'smiley' face, but stopped before adding the eyes and mouth. The circle seemed enough, shimmering faintly on the reflective surface, like a halo.

It was cold and damp outside, a typical February morning in Paris. Somewhere along the line last night, he had lost his scarf; but still, he decided to walk all the way back to his apartment. His head ached, he lifted his eyes upward in search of solace, but the ornate Haussmann buildings had lost their beauty, he felt almost threatened by them, like a commoner surrounded by an aggressive, leering royal court.

He looked up at the sky. It was grey and heavy, like a lead lid, oppressive. He suddenly missed the bright, crisp days of New York City winters. He felt entirely alone, out of place, like a modern character painted incongruously into an ancient canvas.

"It's time to go home," he said out loud.

He hadn't accumulated much in the past few months, a few sweaters, the now lost scarf, some books, nothing more. He could travel light, and fast. Today, even. Despite his exhaustion, he took the stairs up to his apartment two by two and swung open the door purposefully.

Parched from the alcohol and the effort, he went directly into the kitchen to pour himself some water. He saw it immediately. Attached to the fridge, by a promotional magnet that he had gotten for free with a case of beer, was a photograph. It was on regular 8 x 10 white paper, printed off a computer file, the contrast was poor, the image faint, but the content was unmistakable.

The photograph was of a woman's back entirely tattooed with thick, dark blue lines and words. *SHOULDER, LOIN, SPARE RIB, RUMP.*

"Oh my God, Claire. What have you done?"

He sat down on the kitchen floor, the image in his hands.

"You're still in Paris." He sniffed at the air in the apartment like a dog trying to pick up a scent, but there was nothing.

"How could they do that to her? Motherfuckers," he said out loud getting up, the plan to go to every tattoo parlor in town just beginning to form, until, buried deep in his memory he remembered a place near *Les Halles* that they had seen together on their first walk. Dallas had stopped to look at the photographs of freshly tattooed customers that were pasted in the window. He had leaned in close to look at a particular one.

"See that? A fairy holding a cheeseburger…" Dallas had said, "…tattooed on her arm for the rest of her life?! People are nuts."

Peter ran downstairs and past the long line for taxis, he winced at the memory; the metro would be faster anyway. After nearly punching his way through the clerk's window out of frustration at the rigmarole one was put through to obtain one simple metro ticket, muttering "Fucking French!" under his breath he heard the train coming into the station. Shoving people out of the way roughly, he just made it on, the doors grabbing a piece of his jacket as they closed. He yanked it out forcefully, sweating.

He plopped down into a seat. A pretty girl smiled at him. He smiled back reflexively. His breath gradually calmed and he managed to regain some composure. Because he could not will the train forward faster, to distract himself he gazed around the metro car, up at the ads, at the map (five more stops) and finally at the people. His eyes met the girl's again. She looked at him coyly. It irritated him. He shifted his eyes to the very far side of the car, so she would get the message that he wasn't interested.

It must have been something about the angle of the neck, or maybe just a vague familiarity of form. He'd never be sure, but somehow it caught his eye. In the multitude of bobbing heads, way ahead in front of him, through the hats, the shoulders, the thickness of humanity, he discerned a flash of red hair. He narrowed his eyes and could now see that it was shorn very short, cut awkwardly with electric clippers. He got up and walked towards it. The metro was speeding along and he had to steady himself on the metal poles as he made his way over, hand over hand like Tarzan swinging from vine to vine. He stopped directly behind the close-cropped redhead. He braced himself for a moment and finally stepped forward and turned to look at the face.

It was Claire. It was Dallas. It was neither.

He dropped to his knees in front of her and took her limp hands in his, her wrist bones looked like the porcelain handles of his mother's best teacups. She was gazing blindly into the middle distance and didn't seem to notice his touch. She was inexpressibly thin, her skin looked almost translucent, he could see the wavy lines of her veins very clearly. She was wearing a black shirt, black pants, black boots and a black jacket, like Dallas had. He looked at her stomach. The basketball shape was gone.

"Claire."

No answer.

"Claire, my God. Claire, answer me. Look at me."

Nothing. He squeezed her hands tightly.

"Leave me alone," she said hoarsely.

"No. Claire, you need help."

"I don't need any-one or any-thing. I am self-sustaining."

"Claire, you're in trouble. Please let me help you."

People were starting to stare.

"Claire." He lowered his voice, "What happened? What happened to the baby?"

She looked down at her stomach and made a weak 'magician's reveal'-type gesture with her right hand.

"Poof."

"What do you mean, *'poof'*?"

"Just: *Poof*. I woke up one morning and he was gone."

"Who's he? You had a miscarriage?"

"No."

"Claire, focus. What do you mean 'no'?"

"One morning, I woke up and the bump was gone. Gone. I looked everywhere. Really I did, I looked for it everywhere, but it was gone." She became more agitated with each word.

"That's impossible," he reasoned.

She smiled. "I know." And then as if remembering something, she added, "Don't touch me," and pulled her hands away.

Suddenly, as if he'd farted loudly, she snapped her eyes up and looked him straight in the eyes, startled.

"Glory is my daughter," she said simply.

Peter felt a vein in his forehead throb. He had been kneeling, now he leaned back and sat fully on the floor. A woman in a nearby seat got up and moved further down the car.

"I told you I hadn't found her, but I had," she continued simply.

"Claire, this can't be true."

"You always say that, Peter. But it's always true isn't it? No matter how ugly it is, it's always true. You should know that by now."

"Does she know?" Peter managed.

"No."

"Why didn't you tell her?"

"Poor little girl is fucked up enough without knowing where she came from." Claire smiled, gazing blindly ahead. "I just wanted to see her. In fact, I go see her as much as I can. I was there last night."

Peter felt an inexplicably icy, dribble of sweat roll down his back.

"Where? The club? But I looked everywhere for you in the club. You weren't there," he told her.

"I know. I saw you searching. But you were looking for Claire. Maybe even Dallas. Not me."

It was true. In his drunken, agitated state, in the smoky penumbra of the cavernous club, he might not have recognized the person now sitting in front of him as Claire.

"You had sex with my daughter," she said as if she were saying, *'Pass me the salt.'*

Peter's penis tingled at the memory. He pulled at his pant leg involuntarily.

"I didn't know," he answered lamely.

"She's a kid, Peter. What were you thinking?"

He had no answer.

The metro pulled into *Châtelet,* one of the city's major transfer hubs. The doors opened and a flood of people rushed onto the train, nearly trampling him. He stood up awkwardly, his legs, bloodless from the awkward position; he was pushed away from Claire by the throng. At the next station there was another frantic shuffle of people squeezing on and off and he struggled to keep an eye on her through the crowd. He tried again in vain to reach her. The train swerved, a woman accidentally stepped hard on his foot with her stiletto heel, he let out a loud involuntary yelp.

"Oh mon Dieu, je suis vraiment désolée!" the woman apologized profusely.

He looked down at his foot, shook it, and then looked back up at the woman angrily and said, "Fuck you."

The insult left her speechless, her mouth formed into a perfect circle, "O".

He looked back towards Claire, but couldn't see her anymore. He felt a wave of panic and pushed his way fiercely through the crowd. He stared down at the seat she had been in; a fat Moroccan man talking loudly on a cell phone sat in her place.

She was gone.

When the doors opened at the next station he was propelled outwards by the flow of people exiting. He jumped up a few times, like a salmon leaping in a stream. He tried to see above their heads, to find Claire in the crowd. But she wasn't there.

He sat down on one of the red molded plastic seats on the platform and dropped his head into his hands.

He stayed there for hours... At one point an old man dropped a 5€ note into his unconsciously cupped hands. He looked at it and then used it to blow his nose. He had been crying.

He got up, walked up one set of metro stairs and then down another, switching platforms to head back in the direction he had come.

Once on his street, he paused in front of the bar on his corner and looked in the window. He saw the old woman from Tennessee sitting on a barstool, her white hair was tangled and matted; there were flowers in it.

He kept walking down the block. The grey day was turning to night. The streetlights had just come on; they glowed dimly through the fog.

He crossed the narrow street to the front of his building. As he went to punch in the entry code he noticed that the door was propped open. Something was stuck in it. He pushed it open and looked down.

It was Claire's yarn. He felt a surge of hope and followed its trail up the stairs; he pushed open the apartment door and saw that she had tied one end of it to the radiator. He reached down and picked it up. Though initially about a foot wide, stretched out like this, it was narrower. He held it in his right hand at hip height and followed the length of it back down the stairs like a guide rope down a mine.

Once on the street he saw that it ran along the building's base like electrical wire and kept snaking along the lengths of all the buildings on the block. He walked slowly, following it, looking around carefully, hoping she'd emerge from one of the doorways. She did not.

On the corner, he saw that the yarn stretched across the intersection, cars rolled over it. He followed it down the next block slowly, carefully; and then it turned left, hugging the corner of an ornate limestone building they had once admired on one of their walks from home from the Seine.

"Oh no," he whispered. And then shouted involuntarily, "No, no, Claire. NO!"

He started running towards the river. His brain short-circuiting in a tangle of unfamiliar emotion, he stumbled awkwardly, his feet catching each other up as he ran to the small pedestrian bridge he knew was at the end of the street.

Then he saw her.

She was sitting in the middle of the bridge. She had hopped up on its edge like women in Paris often do to facilitate their lover's kiss. Her back was towards the water. He slowed his pace and approached her slowly and cautiously as if befriending an animal in the wild. She didn't move. He finally stood in front of her.

Sitting as she was, they were eye to eye. She was frail, impossibly delicate, like a paper cut-out of herself, yet to him she looked extraordinarily beautiful. Translucent almost, like an eggshell held to the light. She looked right through him, her eyes opaque, flat, but still very, very green. He stepped slightly to the right and leaned his elbows on the bridge's cold, stone lip and looked out onto the water.

He could hear the surprisingly forceful rush of the river below. His ears were cold. So were his hands. He wondered what he could possibly say to convince her to forgive him. To take him back. Perhaps he could apologize, perhaps he could comfort her, perhaps he could tell her that he loved her; nothing seemed right.

"I'm hungry," he finally said, the words forming in his mouth awkwardly, as if he were chewing them.

She didn't respond.

He turned and stood in front of her.

"Did you hear me?" he asked. "Claire, I am hungry. You…I'm…hungry."

Silence; the freezing wind whistled past his ears, it was almost tuneful. On the sleeves of his black coat Peter noticed minute white specks, scattered haphazardly like spilled salt. It was snowing.

"Smoke?" she asked quietly a few moments later.

"What?"

The cold had turned her pale skin an ashy shade of grey. Her lips were blue. He wished he had some crimson lipstick to give her.

"Smoke?" she said again, still staring straight ahead.

He looked at her, not understanding.

She reached into her pocket and handed him something. He took it. He held it between his fingers. It was dry and thin and cigarette shaped. He held it up to the street light questioningly.

It was the leaves. The rolled leaves.

"Oh, Claire," he said, his voice soft.

"Do you have a lighter?" she asked.

He couldn't take his eyes off her. "Yes."

"Let's smoke it together."

"Claire, I real…"

"Please." And then more quietly, "please."

He put the tight roll of leaves to his mouth and lit it. He inhaled deeply in an effort to please her. Surprisingly, it tasted sweet. After his drag he handed it to her. She took it carefully between her frail fingers and took a small puff and coughed; she wasn't used to smoking.

He smiled at her. The wind picked up again, as he pulled his collar tighter around his neck, he noticed her swaying a little, forward and back, just slightly, like a long flower in a light summer breeze. Then in one graceful motion she arched backwards; precisely, like a gymnast. Her body in the shape of a comma, she edited herself definitively out of the moment, and into the void.

He rushed forward to see her do a flip as graceful as the one she had done the night the car had hit her head on.

Without a moment's hesitation, he dove in after her; yanked almost, as if an invisible rope was tied between them. Falling headfirst, he thought he saw a circle form, for an infinitesimal instant, on the frothy surface before the water engulfed him with a choking rush.

In the depths, he opened his eyes, it was brighter than he expected. Reaching, grabbing frantically in front of him and behind, he searched for her. Nothing.

A rich smell he couldn't define suddenly enveloped him. Magnolia? Vomit? Honey? He turned.

There she was.

Deep under the water, in its hushed silence, he grabbed her shoulders. She grabbed his. They looked into each other's eyes for a long time. Their hearts slowed to a gentle rhythm; the soft, satisfying *clip-clop* of perfectly matched partners hitting tennis balls back and forth on a warm summer afternoon.

Claire smiled. Her teeth glowed, white.

Eventually, and quite by surprise, they both heard a muted 'click'.

It was the sound of the world snapping into place.

Post Script

In September of 2004, while on a walk around Paris, a single sentence popped into my head: *Peter never ate*. Insistent, it kept coming back again and again, in an effort to dissipate it; I put it to paper. The three words called out to me from the page. The short sentence was like some sort of motor, of magnet. I touched my pen back to the paper and let it lead me over the course of a few months, sentence by sentence until I had written enough sentences to cover over 60 pages. Those pages are the first half of the book you have just read.

Now, what's interesting about this is not that I wrote over 60 pages; it's how I wrote those pages. I wrote them unconsciously. Yes, I know…that's impossible. So, obviously I wasn't literally unconscious, but I wasn't using what I consider my conscious mind to write. In other words, I had never written a book before, I didn't have a plot or outline, characters sketched or any idea at all what I was going to write about. I would just get myself to a quiet place, read the last paragraph I had written and then just pick up where I had left off and keep writing until it felt natural to stop; sometimes it was an hour, sometimes it was 8 hours. It was a strange, invigorating, and somewhat frightening experience.

After those initial 60 pages, life intruded and I put them aside to go back to a daily job. But the experience had changed me. I started expressing myself much more freely in writing of all kinds, I started a blog, wrote some articles. But it just wasn't the same feeling. A few years later I found myself with a chunk of free time, I dug out the pages and shared them with a friend who vehemently encouraged me to 'finish' the book. How could I 'finish' what I hadn't even consciously started? After putting it off for a few weeks, I gathered my courage and sat down to write. Lo and behold – it happened again. My conscious brain clicked off, something else clicked on, and the second half of what was to become *Gag* surged forth.

I tried to explain the sensation to a friend, and the closest I came to expressing it correctly was by saying that it felt like I was driving in a car on a dark road with no idea where I was or where I was going, but I had the headlights on and could just see enough to stay on the road. I would look ahead into the little illuminated patch of ground and keep inching forward. My sense of time was completely altered when I was writing, a whole day could go by in what felt like an hour. Words gushed out of me like an open faucet.

The next day he emailed me a television interview of the French author Patrick Mondiano. When asked how he wrote, he described my experience, verbatim. I knew in that instant that I had experienced the elusive 'flow'. I had been fortunate enough to accidentally tap into what I now believe is an innate source of creativity that exists in us all.

I believe that when I sat down to write that first day I wasn't held back by fear or other typical blocks because I didn't consider myself 'an author' nor did I particularly yearn to be – I had nothing to 'prove' or to 'lose', so the words just flowed out untainted by my critical conscious mind. And that was the day that changed my life forever.

For those of you who feel something stirring within you, I hope that having read this book and the story of how it came into being will encourage you to express yourself creatively in a manner unhindered by any conscious boundaries or codes. Relax. Good or bad does not exist, those are subjective terms, reach toward authenticity instead. I have come to believe that our truest voice can be found in creative activities in which we release rational thought and allow something other than our conscious mind to fill in the blanks.

I know this isn't big news. I don't purport to put forth any new or groundbreaking philosophical ideas. I just hope to encourage you to take the time to ignite your inner spark. *Scintilla animae* as it's called so poetically in Latin.

My greatest wish is to inspire you to tap into your imagination, explore your subconscious and to shout your soul through your fingertips.

What I felt writing these pages was the nearest to a state of grace that I have experienced in my lifetime and I wish that experience for everyone.

Melissa Unger
Paris, France
January 2014

Acknowledgments

The gratitude I owe to my friends is unfathomable. Throughout the years this extraordinary group of individuals has inspired, helped and protected me in the most loving and heroic manner possible. Collectively, they are the very definition of generosity. Thank you, each and every one of you.

Merci mille fois to Kéran Masselin; living by his side has made me a better human being.

My deepest thanks to my mother, Valerie Unger and my father, Sy Unger who set me off on this magnificent and fascinating journey; thank you for inviting me into the world.

About the Author

Melissa Unger is a writer, creative consultant and the founder of Seymour Projects.

She has spent the past 25 years working with individuals and organizations from a wide variety of creative fields. She began her career production managing music videos after which she worked as a production assistant on a number of feature films including: *A Bronx Tale, Quiz Show, The Age Of Innocence*. She has been the personal assistant to both *Daniel Day Lewis* and *Robert De Niro*. She has also held posts at *Jumbo Pictures*, the *Ad Council* and *Galerie Thaddaeus Ropac* and has consulted for a number of artists and arts-related organizations including *artnet* and the *Creative Growth Art Center.*

In 2011, she founded Seymour Projects. Seymour offers multidisciplinary projects that motivate people to take regular breaks from technology to relax their mind, explore their subconscious, cultivate their imagination & uncover their authentic creative voice.

Born in New York City, she currently resides in Paris, France. *Gag* is Melissa Unger's first book.
www.seymourprojects.com

ROUNDFIRE
BOOKS